MW01134349

OBSESSIVE RAGE

The Sycamore File

Ryan Stevenson
and
Richard Brandeis

ISBN-13: 978-1530836697
ISBN-10: 1530836697

PRINTED IN THE UNITED STATES OF AMERICA

This book is dedicated to the thousands of men and women in the medical profession that have given their time and knowledge in the pursuit of understanding the human mind.

CONTENTS

PREFACE

Although the exact cause of most mental illnesses is not known, it is becoming clear through research that many of these conditions are caused by a combination of genetic, biological, psychological, and environmental factors—not personal weakness or a character defect; therefore, recovery from a mental illness is not simply a matter of will and self-discipline.

It is to the thousands of professional men and women in the fields of Psychotherapy and Psychiatry, as well as those in Law Enforcement, who work tirelessly to treat and protect those suffering from mental illness, that this fictional account is dedicated.

PROLOGUE

I had just finished reading my latest issue of *JAMA Psychiatry*, and a particular article brought back memories of one of the most bizarre cases I ever had to handle while I was a first year psychiatric resident. Bellevue Hospital in New York saw its fair share of cases, but I'll never forget that early fall evening as long as I live.

There isn't any question that the human brain, from a structural perspective, is very much understood. It's the exquisite balance of our brain's chemistry coupled with human emotion that we still have to understand, and after dealing with this one noteworthy patient, I wondered if medical science ever would.

This particular patient, in laymen's terms, simply snapped. It was a complete and total psychotic break with reality, yet it is what happened after the patient literally lost his mind. It is events like this that keep professionals like me up at night, along with law enforcement personnel.

Chapter 1

Summers in the south were always incredibly hot. Momma had always said if I wanted baked apples, I could just set them out on the sidewalk and let the sun do the rest. It's August of 1933, and I know the depression has taken its toll on everyone, from the richest of the rich to the poorest of the poor. Here in Atlanta, life seemed to be even more bitter, as people wandered the streets looking for handouts. Those brave men that came back and prospered after World War I were now barely able to make a living. Travelers in cars from the northern states, heading south to look for work, would run out of gas as well as money. They would leave their cars on the side of the road only to allow time and the weather to turn their dreams of a new future into rust and heartbreak.

Dad passed away years ago from the Spanish influenza, and living with my mother in a rundown wood frame house with railroad tracks in the rear allowed me to watch hobos jump from a train if they felt this was their stop. As I sat in my room on one of our famously hot, steamy nights, the 9:35-train from up north was slowing down, and men of all colors, shapes and sizes began to disembark.

One man looked up to my window and asked if I had any food for an old soldier. All I could suggest was to try the local Baptist Mission on South Street. "They may still have some soup and bread available," I said. He thanked me and went on his way.

With so many strangers around, there really wasn't much one could do other than stay close to home. Several young girls had been murdered over in another county, and Momma told me never to stray far from home.

Momma was our church organist, but she had learned to play the piano first. She always said I had the voice of an angel, and every night after dinner we both would retire to the parlor, where Momma would play Christian hymns while I sang along.

One evening after the dinner dishes were washed and placed back in the cupboard, Momma said, "Lila, it's time to warm up that angelic voice of yours."

"Sure, Momma," I said. "Just let me open the window so we get some air in this place."

Momma would always start our singing session with *Be Thou My Vision.* It was one of her favorites. As I sang, out of the corner of my eye, I noticed a young man who couldn't have been more than thirty-five, standing across the street. I had never seen this man before. He was dressed in what appeared to be a rumpled old suit, just standing there, listening to the music waft through the heavy steam-laden air. Maybe it was my voice that gave the man pause to stop and listen.

"Pay attention, Lila," Momma cautioned, and I turned away for the briefest of moments, but when I looked back out the window, the young man had moved on.

Chapter 2

It was going to be another scorcher of a day. Momma had errands to run and told me to stay close to home. We had a small wooden porch that had seen better days, but at least the chair swing that my father had built years ago still served its purpose. I would glide back and forth, just trying to catch even the faintest of breezes to cool off. At the age of twenty-three, there wasn't much for a young southern woman to do other than to get married off, but there wasn't anyone special in my life. So I stayed with Momma, never really knowing what the next day might bring. It was kind of accepted as the southern way of doing things.

I was reading a month-old newspaper, *The Times Courier*, just wondering if the police had caught whoever had strangled those poor girls Momma had told me about. Other than listening to what I could hear from a neighbor's radio, there wasn't much in the way of news on that terrible tragedy over in Bucks County.

The heat of the day was getting oppressive, so I decided to make some lemonade in the hope of cooling off. Then the strangest feeling came over me as I stood over the sink filling Momma's favorite pitcher with water. It was almost as if I could feel a pair of eyes staring at me, yet to the best of my knowledge, there wasn't a soul around. I had never experienced that sudden chill before, along with goose bumps on my arms in the Georgia heat, but there they were.

I noticed Momma had forgotten to dump the drip pan under the icebox, so I took care of that, and no sooner had I finished, than there was a knock on the front door. Mr. Gibbons ran the local ice house, and right on time he had arrived to deliver a block of ice that would last us a week. Momma must have known he was going to deliver, as she had left me a shiny quarter on the kitchen table to pay Mr. Gibbons, just in case he showed up.

Sam Gibbons was truly a southern gentleman, inasmuch as he brought the block of ice in the house and then took it down stairs to the cellar, where he broke it up into smaller pieces that were used during the week. I paid Sam, and with a tip of his hat, he was on his way to the next house up the street. It wasn't long after Sam had left that Momma returned from her errands.

To make a few dollars here and there, Momma and I would take in sewing, or do laundry for a few folks in the neighborhood. It wasn't much, but just enough so that we could eat. I would ask Momma when I could get out of the house and maybe help out making some money at anything I could find.

"Until those murders are solved, Young Lady, you're not going anywhere," she said.

Chapter 3

Momma had stopped at the local butcher and brought home a ham shank that barely had any meat left on the bone. But I swear, Momma could create a five-star meal with what little we had in the pantry, and a full stomach never gives a person these days anything to complain about.

Momma got that ham shank in exchange for washing the butcher's white aprons that were usually covered with blood stains, sweat, and Lord knows what else. She handed me the bundle and said, "Lila, you start washing these, and I'll get dinner going for us."

I grabbed the bundle of dirty aprons and went out back where we had an old pump well and a large wooden tub. As I was filling the tub getting ready to wash the aprons, that very strange feeling came over me again and sent a chill down my spine. All I could sense was that there was someone from a distance staring at me, and yet I didn't see a soul around. Then again, anyone would have to be half crazy to be out in this summer heat. I couldn't explain the feeling I was having, and when it happened the second time, I still brushed it off. I must have been just letting my imagination run away with me.

After I finished the wash, I dumped the water out of the tub and set it up on its side against the rear of the house. There must have been at least a dozen aprons that I hung out to dry on the clothesline, securing each one with two clothespins. Then, as I began walking back toward the house, I spotted that man in the rumpled suit walking slowly down the street, looking in my direction.

I tried not to make eye contact and walked pretty fast back into the house, locking the back door behind me. I thought this was the same man that had stood across the street the evening before while Momma played and I sang. Was it just coincidence that this stranger was still in the neighborhood? It just seemed so odd to me, since I knew everyone on our street, so I wondered who this stranger might be.

I never mentioned any of this to Momma, as I didn't want to upset her. I just figured I would wait another day or two to talk to her, rather than let my imagination play tricks on me.

So many displaced people traveling in every which direction just amazed me. You couldn't mistake the downtrodden men who once could have been the head of their own companies, now out of work and panhandling for food, barely surviving with just the clothes they had on their backs. Every time I saw these men jump from the train, probably thinking this time they would find work, I couldn't help but sense that feeling of loss. Lost lives, lost loves, and broken families. The Great Depression was taking its toll on everyone in the country.

Chapter 4

After the laundry was taken care of and hung up to dry, I returned to the kitchen to see if Momma needed any help getting dinner ready.

"Lila, just set the table. The rice is almost ready and we'll eat soon."

"Momma, can I ask you a question?"

"Yes, Lila. What's on your mind, Child?"

Momma, I'm twenty-three years old. Do you think I can take care of myself?" I asked.

"Now where is this nonsense coming from, Lila?" Momma asked.

"Well, Momma, I think I'm old enough to get out of this house and help you. I could go around town and see if I can get more washing from people. At least it would bring in a bit more money."

Momma looked at me with a whimsical smile and said, "Child, I've tried keeping you safe all these years, but sooner or later I knew you would want to spread your wings. Why don't we do this, Lila? You can leave the house to see if you can drum up a bit more business for us, but only during the day; you better get your knickers back here before the sun sets. I don't want you outside any later until the police solve the murders of those two girls. God bless their souls".

"Do you really mean that, Momma?" I asked.

"Yes, Lila, I do. It was going to happen sooner or later

and it's not like we can't use a few extra dollars."

"Thank you, Momma, for placing your trust in me. I won't let you down".

For the first time in my life I actually felt that I had won some level of freedom in being able to venture outside. Dinner was nearly ready, and on this night I would sing my heart out. After dinner, we cleaned up and headed to the parlor as we always did. The sun was just falling below the horizon, and after opening the window, Momma sat at the piano and began playing *Amazing Grace.*

As I began to sing along, I again felt as if someone was looking in my direction, and there, across the street, was that young man I had seen the night before. Who was this man and why was he standing outside our house for the second night in a row? I tried not to look in his direction, but couldn't help myself.

Momma said, "Pay attention, Lila." And with that, I glimpsed at the young man and smiled for a split second before Momma asked what I seemed all fussy about outside the window.

"It's nothing, Momma," and then I thought, *Maybe I have a secret admirer.*

We finished our session for the night, ending with *Great Is Thy Faithfulness.* Momma was very tired and wanted to retire for the evening.

"You go on up to bed, Momma," I said. "I'll set out the plates for breakfast and then turn in myself".

After Momma left the parlor, I walked over to the window, and again, the young man had vanished. I thought to myself, *Maybe he's a big time music agent that wants to whisk me off to Hollywood to become a star.* But reality set in just as fast. His clothes had seen better days and I was only kidding myself in thinking that he was a man of any means.

As I got ready for bed, I sat in front of my mirror, brushing my hair. All I could think of was having a chance meeting with the stranger who stood outside my window. I wasn't sure what I might say, but he must love Christian hymns if he felt it necessary to stand outside listening to me sing.

Chapter 5

Morning arrived with a clap of thunder that woke me up out of a sound sleep. The streets were still hot from the day before, and with each drop of rain that fell, you could feel the steam rising from the ground. Summer storms didn't last very long, and today was going to be my first day in trying to drum up a little more business for Momma and me.

The plumbing in the house must have dated back to the 1800's when the house was built, and every time you turned on the water faucet, you would have to let it run for a few minutes just to clear the pipes of rust. We didn't have a shower, only a tub. Since I wanted to get out of the house as soon as I could, I skipped a bath and just wet a towel and began to wipe away the sweat.

I tied my hair back in a ponytail, slipped on some clothes, and set out to see what new business I might be able to get. As I walked out of my room and closed the door, I heard something fall in my room. I turned around and opened the door again to my room, and there was a large piece of plaster that had fallen off the wall. *Land sakes,* I thought to myself. *If this place stands another year I will truly be surprised.* I swept up the plaster that had fallen on the floor and decided to wait until later to talk to Momma about it, since I was in a hurry to get going.

I went downstairs and found Momma already in the kitchen, making some of her fresh biscuits while heating up some gravy that was left over from the night before. "You're up early Lila," she said to me. "Excited about the day, are we?"

"Yes, Momma, I am. I'm going to find us some new customers and won't take *no* for an answer."

"Well, Lila, I'm going to deliver the aprons we washed last night to the butcher, and then I have to run over to see Mr. Hollis at the Woolworth Five and Dime Store. I heard they may be looking for counter help."

"Oh Momma, that would be wonderful if you can get a job like that," I said.

"Wish me luck, Lila, and we'll see what happens."

"Momma, I just know I'm going to make you proud. Don't you worry, Momma. I'm going to find some new customers for us."

After eating breakfast, I left Momma behind and began my journey through some of the more commercial streets in Atlanta. I just figured that there had to be people who owned a business that needed something cleaned. The sun was getting higher in the sky and you could begin to feel the heat rising from the streets.

I spotted Johnny Rae Crawford's bakery and decided that would be a good place to start. As I walked in, the woman behind the counter asked if she could help me.

"I would like to talk to Mr. Crawford, if you don't mind, Mam" I replied.

"Is this personal?" the woman asked.

"Not rightly so, Mam, but it is important. Is he available?" I asked.

The woman walked to the back of the store and there he was, as big as life. *He must love eating what he bakes,* I thought to myself.

"Yes, Miss, I'm the owner, Mr. Crawford. How may I help you?"

"Well Sir, no doubt you know times are tough, and I've been trying to help my momma by picking up and washing laundry. We both do a really good job and never have had any complaints. I was wondering, Mr. Crawford, if there was something that you might need cleaned on a daily or weekly basis?"

"Well, Young Lady, we already have most of our uniforms and towels and aprons, done at the local laundry, and they only charge us five cents apiece for each item. They also pick up and deliver like clockwork."

"Mr. Crawford, if you give me the chance to show you what I can do, and even cheaper than the laundry and just as clean, would you consider giving me some of your items on a trial basis?"

Mr. Crawford seemed interested, and looking at me through glasses coated with flour dust, he asked, "Just how much do you charge for this service, Young Lady?"

I paused for a moment, then said, "Mr. Crawford, I will clean any item just as well as the laundry does for just two cents apiece, and you can try my service for one week. If you're happy then, I would consider we have a deal."

"OK, I will try you out, but for one week only," Mr. Crawford said. "If your service is as good as you say it is, you can have all of my business, seeing that I can save three cents on each item and put the money to better use. You have a deal, Young Lady."

"Oh thank you, Mr. Crawford. I promise you won't be disappointed. If you would get anything you want cleaned and bundled for me, I'll be back in a few minutes and pick up what you have."

With that, I headed out the door and ran as fast as I could back to the house for my old Red Flyer wagon, so I could carry Mr. Crawford's laundry back to the house. This was going to be a red-letter day for Momma and me.

Chapter 6

When I got back home, I ran around the back of the house to fetch my wagon. It wasn't very big, but at least it had wheels, and I wouldn't have to drag Mr. Crawford's laundry through the streets. I headed back to the bakery with my wagon, and left it out in front of the store. As promised, Mr. Crawford had two large bundles ready for me, and even helped me load them onto my wagon.

"You'll have these back in three days, Mr. Crawford, and you won't be sorry," I said.

As I headed back home, one of the bundles kept falling off the wagon, and I would have to stop each time and pick it up before I could get going again. The third time this happened, as I stooped to pick up the bundle, I was startled when I felt a hand taking hold of mine. When I looked up, I saw a man bending over me, who asked: "May I help you, Young Lady?"

It took only a moment for me to realize that this man was the same person that had stood outside my window for two nights listening to me sing.

"Thank you, Sir, but I think I can manage. Besides, I never talk to strangers."

"Well, I can't be much of a stranger since you have been serenading me for the last two nights," he smiled.

“Still and all, Mister, I think I can manage,” I said. “Sorry, I have to go.”

As I began to walk away, I just had a feeling he wasn't from these parts; he sounded as if he were from up north. Maybe I was just being a little apprehensive, considering that the murder of those two girls hadn't been solved yet, but I did think that maybe I should have been a little nicer to him. I stopped for a moment, then turned around to ask the man where he had come from, but he was nowhere to be seen. It didn't matter at this point, since I had work to do and wanted to make Momma proud.

I finally got back home and pulled my wagon with the two bundles around to the back of the house. As I opened the first bundle, I began to take a count of everything that was there. Twenty towels, fifteen aprons, twenty-five smaller hand towels, and twenty baker’s uniforms. By my count, after washing these items, I would make one dollar and sixty cents, and I hadn't even opened the second bundle yet. As I began to fill the tub, I grabbed the soap, bleach, and a brush, and got started. It took me about an hour to get the first load finished and hung, and then I tackled the second bundle.

Let's see. Thirty more towels, twenty aprons, and fourteen smaller towels. This batch would be well over a dollar as well. I just knew Momma would be proud of me, and we surely could use the extra money.

By my count at two cents apiece, I would make two dollars and eighty-eight cents, and considering the heat outside, everything would be dried by sunset. Then I would bring everything into the house and fold every item. I wanted to make sure that Mr. Crawford was pleased with his new laundry service, so I had decided to get everything washed and dried first, rather than going out looking for any more business. Considering what Momma made doing laundry, we now could really eat in style any time we had a mind to.

Chapter 7

It didn't take me more than three hours to get everything washed, and in the summer Georgia sun, the clothes were dry lickety-split. I brought everything into the house and began folding each item on the kitchen table. All the uniforms in one pile, towels in another, and then I used some of Momma's kitchen twine to tie up each bundle, and wrapped them all in brown paper. I thought to myself, *I'll bet that isn't something a commercial laundry does for their clients.*

It wasn't long before Momma arrived back home, and when she walked into the kitchen, her legs nearly buckled. "Child, where in the world did all this laundry come from?" she asked.

"Well, Momma, I stopped at the bakery and spoke to Mr. Crawford, and asked if I could do any of his laundry. He said he was being charged five cents apiece, and when I told him I would do it for two cents an item he jumped at the thought of saving money. Are you happy, Momma? Because I have just made us two dollars and eighty-eight cents."

"My word, Lila, I never would have imagined this happening at all. I guess we're going to have to buy more soap powder and bleach to keep up with the demand."

I knew Momma would be happy, and best of all I could go shopping for some of the foods we never could afford before. "Glad you're happy, Momma. I'm going to surprise

Mr. Crawford and use my old wagon to deliver his items tomorrow. I told him I would be back in three days, so I think he'll be surprised to get them early."

"He sure will, Lila!" Momma exclaimed.

Momma said to go get cleaned up, as she would have dinner ready in a few minutes. I knew she was proud of me, and for the first time in a long time, we actually looked like we would have more money coming in rather than going out.

I was really tired after doing all that laundry, and the bleach I had used was really bothering my hands. So I went upstairs to the bathroom, and after allowing the rusty water to return clear, I soaked my hands just to make sure all the bleach had washed off.

As I headed back downstairs, I heard Momma talking to someone at the front door. It sounded like a gentleman's voice, and as I drew closer, I knew I recognized the sound of his voice. It was the stranger who tried helping me in the street; the same man in the rumpled suit. I didn't stand around listening, but walked back into the kitchen. When Momma returned, I asked who was at the door.

"Lila, it was just a man from up north that has fallen on hard times, like so many other people in the country. He asked if I might have had anything extra to eat, and since you had finished the last of the biscuits this morning, I had to turn him away."

"Oh," I said, "we do see a lot of people that probably go hungry everyday."

"You know, Lila, millions of people have placed their faith in President Roosevelt. He talks about creating all kinds of work programs, but the south always seems to get the short end of the stick. The government seems more interested in building national parks that no one can afford to get to, when what we really need here are jobs."

"I know, Momma, but maybe President Roosevelt will bring some of those jobs down here. This dang depression can't last forever."

"Well, it sure seems like it has, but now that we have a little extra income, maybe things will get better for us before long," she said.

I never did mention to Momma that the man she was talking to was the same man that had tried helping me in the street on the way home. I didn't think it would make much difference anyway, so I just forgot about it.

Chapter 8

After we finished what was left of the ham shank, along with some rice and beans, we cleaned up and headed for the parlor for a little music. As Momma warmed up on the piano, I peeked outside to see if that stranger was still hanging around, but there wasn't a trace of him.

"Momma, how about we try something a little different this evening?"

"What do you mean *different*, Lila?"

"Well, Momma, instead of hymns, do you know that new song Mr. Bing Crosby has been singing? I think it's called *Please*."

"Child, I will not have that trash music in this house. We've always sung hymns and I'm not about to change now."

"Oh please, Momma," I begged.

"No, Lila, that music belongs in bars and saloons, and not in a southern Christian home, and that's final."

"Okay, Momma, but would it really hurt to try something a little different once in a while?"

As Momma got up from the piano I saw the tears in her eyes when she pulled an old lace handkerchief from her belt that she was wearing around her waist.

"What's wrong, Momma?" I asked.

"Lila, since your father passed away, I've tried raising you in a decent Christian home. While you live here, I need you to understand that I will not have that crazy music in this house. None other than Satan himself created that noise, and I just won't have it in my home."

"Okay, Momma, I understand, and won't ask again."

Momma then left to go to her bedroom, and I could still hear her muffled sobbing as she climbed the stairs.

What little electric we had in the past had been turned off a long time ago because we just couldn't pay the bill, so we had to resort to kerosene lamps. I lowered the wicks on all the lamps downstairs to extinguish the flames—all except the one in the parlor, which I brought up to my room.

The Great Depression had hit the country broadside. Millions were out of work; stocks that once soared were now worthless pieces of paper. The days of speakeasies and flappers were over, and now some felt the need just to jump out of windows. There was a dust bowl forming in the Midwest, and every so often, if the wind were strong enough, topsoil from the plains would blow toward the east coast and darken the skies.

As I sat on my bed, I prayed to God for help in lifting our great country out of this terrible depression. Sometimes I even wondered if there really was a God, or if there was, why He was letting this happen to so many people. But Momma had always kept the faith, and always said that better days were on the way.

I was trying to do my part to help by taking on some extra laundry, and at least I knew that tomorrow would be a slightly brighter day after giving Mr. Crawford my bill for his laundry. After spending what scant money we had for food, it just seemed that there was little, if anything, left over for even the smallest pleasure, like a five-cent ice cream cone at the drug store.

But I knew if I worked hard, even after paying for additional soap and bleach, maybe one day I would be able to have just the smallest of delights all to myself.

Chapter 9

When the following morning arrived, I was excited to get my day going so I could deliver Mr. Crawford's laundry before the three days was up when I had promised it would be done. It was only 6:30 in the morning, but light enough to see. The air seemed unusually heavy for this time of the day, but then again, this was the deep south, and summers here were borderline intolerable.

This was going to be a great day, and without missing a beat, I quietly went downstairs while Momma was still sleeping. I wrote her a note saying I was going to deliver Mr. Crawford's laundry and would be right back.

I picked up the wrapped bundles of laundry and placed them neatly in my wagon and off I went. The city was just beginning to come to life, and with each block I walked, street lamps began to dim and then go out. It was a new day, and nothing was going to get in my way of delivering Mr. Crawford's laundry.

I knew that the bakery opened promptly at seven a.m., but I was sure that Mr. Crawford was probably there even earlier, with his workers, getting ready for another day. The streets were almost empty and the only sign of life was the milk-delivery man, with his horse-drawn wagon making deliveries to different businesses on the street.

As I drew closer to the bakery, I could feel my heart pounding in my chest, anticipating the reaction that Mr.

Crawford would have when he saw I had finished his job two days early. As I pulled my wagon to his front door, I saw a sign up saying the store was closed.

This couldn't be possible, as they always opened at seven promptly. I tapped on the door, and when the door opened, there stood a surprised Mr. Crawford. "Lila," he said, "what in the world are you doing here at this time of day?"

"Well, Mr. Crawford, you're my largest client and I wanted to make sure that we got off on the right foot. So rather than taking three days to complete your job, I finished everything for you in twenty four hours, separated all of the items, bundled them, and here they are."

The look on his face was one of amazement as he held the door open for me while I rolled my wagon into his store.

"Well, Lila, this is remarkable. Let's take a look."

He may have tried holding back his smile as he opened each package I gave him, but his eyes lit up in amazement. "How in the world did you ever accomplish this in so short a time?" he asked."

"Just good old American knowhow," I replied. "Are you satisfied with the quality of my work?"

"Lila, these came out perfect, and I'm happy to say that you now have my account for as long as you wish. How much do I owe you for your service?"

"Two dollars and eighty-eight cents, Mr. Crawford," I replied.

"Lila, that's the best two dollars and eighty-eight cents I've ever spent. Now make sure you're back here next Monday, and I'll have the next load ready for you."

"Thank you, Mr. Crawford. You made a wise choice in using my laundry service, and you won't be disappointed."

"Lila, if this is the quality of your work, I know I'm in good hands," Mr. Crawford said. He was still smiling from ear to ear when he opened the door for me as I left his store.

I walked as fast as I could to get back home to surprise Momma, and just as I approached the house, I saw Momma waiting at the front door. I reached into my right pocket and handed her the money I had made. Momma was a proud and strong-willed woman, but I could see the tears well up in her eyes when I handed her the money from Mr. Crawford.

I went around the back of the house and dropped off my wagon and then joined Momma in the kitchen for a cup of coffee.

"Are you Okay, Momma?" I asked."

"I'm so proud of you, Lila. I know I may have been a little hard on you last night, so what would you say to our doing a little celebrating?"

"Momma, why don't we just save the extra money for now, and I'll get a few more accounts before this day is over."

"Lila, that's a great idea. I have to pick up some shirts at Judge Johnston's home and should be back by lunch time."

"Okay, Momma, I'll meet you back here then. I want to get out early and start knocking on a few doors this morning, and now I can even use Mr. Crawford as a reference." "

"That sounds wonderful, Lila. We'll get together then. Now you be safe, and please be careful of strangers. There seems to be more and more of them walking the streets these days."

"I'll be safe, Momma. Don't you worry about me."

Chapter 10

Momma left the house, and I was getting ready to leave myself, but I had thought about what she had said about the possibility of getting a job that opened up down at the Woolworth store. I knew I had the account for Mr. Crawford, and with just a few more accounts like that we would be on easy street.

I left the house and walked around the neighborhood looking for any company that might be able to use my services. I stopped at several places, including a grocery store, a plumbing supply store, and even an auto garage, but no one seemed interested. Maybe this just wasn't my day, so I decided to head back to the house to meet up with Momma. By the time I returned home Momma was already back from picking up Judge Johnston's dress shirts, which I could take care of later in the day.

“How did it go, Momma, with the job opening at the Woolworth store?” I asked.

Momma's face turned kind of glum, and before she said a word, I knew she didn't get the position.

“Well, Lila, I asked about the opening, and the manager said he didn't think I was the right person for the job.”

“What was the position, Momma?” I asked.

“It was working behind the lunch counter. Maybe he was just looking for someone younger, but Lord knows I tried.”

"Momma, don't you worry. We have our laundry business to fall back on until something better comes along."

That got me to thinking. I excused myself and went up to my room to change into my one and only dress that I had just cleaned for our upcoming Sunday service, and when I came back downstairs, Momma asked why I had changed.

"I think I'm going to try and get a few more accounts for us, Momma. I'll be back before you even miss me," I said.

"All right, Lila. You be careful now, you hear me?"

"Yes, Momma, I hear you." And out the door I flew.

There really was only one place I was headed, and that was to the Woolworth store that had turned Momma down for the counter position. I was wearing a white dress with faded yellow roses printed on it, but before walking into the store I slapped both of my cheeks so they would be nice and red. It kind of made me look like I had on some blush.

I walked into the store and asked the woman at the register if I could talk to the manager. She pointed out where he was standing, and I began to walk in his direction. I must have been within ten feet of him when he turned and seemed startled to see me.

"Well, Young Lady, that is an awfully pretty dress you have on. Is there something I can help you with?" he asked.

"Well, Sir, yes there is," I replied.

"No need to be formal, Darlin'. My name is *Horace*, and I'm the manager of this here store. Now how may I help you?"

"Well, Horace, my name is *Lila Hartley*, and I noticed you have had a sign in the window for some time now looking for an employee to work behind the lunch counter, and I wanted to apply for the position," I said.

Horace looked at me every which way from Sunday, and then asked: "Have you ever worked as a server, Lila?"

"I can't rightly say I have, but I do learn quickly, and I am a really hard worker and won't mind any hours I might have to work."

While I waited for his reply, Horace just kept staring at me, especially at my chest, which made me feel uncomfortable.

"I'll tell you what, Lila—I'm willing to take a chance with you. But rather than have you serve, I would like for you to work the cash register at the end of the counter. The job pays five dollars a week, if you're interested."

"Yes, Sir, I mean *Horace*, I'll take it. When can I start?"

"You be here at eight a.m. tomorrow morning, and that woman over yonder will train you on the register. And do me a favor, Darlin'. On your way out, could you just remove that help-wanted sign from the window and throw it in the trash."

"Thank you, Horace, for having faith in me. I won't let you down, and I will be here bright and early tomorrow."

I shook Horace's hand and thanked him again as I made my way to the front of the store to remove the sign. I couldn't believe my ears when he said he would pay me five whole dollars a week, and I knew that Momma would be so happy that more money would be coming in.

Chapter 11

After I got rid of the help-wanted sign, I rushed as fast as I could to get back home and give Momma the good news. I was walking so fast that as I turned a corner I ran right into a man who was coming from the opposite direction.

"Oh, I'm so sorry I bumped into you, Mister."

Then suddenly I realized it was the same young man in the old suit that had been standing outside my window as I was singing. In spite of his old clothes, I noticed that he had a very handsome face; and as his strong arms grabbed mine, he held me at arm's length and asked: "Well now, Young Lady, where are you going in such a hurry?"

"Well, if you must know, I just came from a job interview at the Five and Dime Store, and I'll start working there tomorrow."

"Really now, you don't say."

"Yes, I do say. And now I have to be going. By the way, Mister, you're not from around these parts, are you?" I asked.

"I do have a name, Young Lady. It's *Charles.* And no, I'm not from around these parts."

"Well, Charles, maybe we can talk some other time, but I have to get going now."

"May I ask what your name is?" he asked.

"Why, my name is *Lila*, and I really do have to get on my way.

"Maybe we can talk another time then, Lila."

"Just maybe we can, Charles."

I then backed up a step or two and walked around Charles to get on my way. As I continued on to the house, I kind of felt sorry for Charles. He probably had lost a job or a business up north, and may have hit the road like so many men that were looking for work. But I couldn't worry about that now, as I was anxious to share the good news I had about getting the job. I just knew Momma would be so happy with the extra money we would have coming in now.

By the time I had made it back to our house, Mamma was sitting on the porch swing, catching up on some sewing for a neighbor. "Lila, were you able to get any other laundry accounts this afternoon?" she asked, as I joined her on the porch.

"Well, not exactly, Momma," I said.

"And what does *not exactly* mean, Child?"

"Momma, you know that job you tried to get at the Woolworth store working behind the counter?"

"Yes, of course. What about it?"

"Well, Momma, I spoke to the manager there and I didn't get that job either."

"It seems like there's always a black cloud following this family, Lila," Momma commented, sadly.

"I know, Momma, it was a real crying shame I didn't get that job. But guess what! He did offer to train me on the register, and is willing to pay me five dollars a week, and I start tomorrow at eight a.m."

Momma looked up from her glasses and from all appearances seemed to be in shock. "Lila, you mean you got the job I applied for?" she asked.

"No, Momma, not the counter job you wanted. This is a job at the register, ringing up customers after they have eaten and are ready to pay. But who cares what the job is? It's going to bring in another five dollars a week, and we sure can use the money."

Momma looked down at her hands and then looked up again and said, "I just want you to know I am so proud of you, Lila. But now that you have Mr. Crawford's laundry account, who is going to take care of that?"

"I will, Momma, if I have to work day and night to get it done. Or we could split the laundry between us."

"You know, Lila, now with your new job, between the two of us we could be making more than ten dollars a week. Praise the Lord, Child. We're in high cotton now. Maybe those dark clouds are just beginning to part for us," she said.

"I knew you would be happy, Momma, and I can't wait to get started. I'm just going to go up to my room and get out of my Sunday dress, and then I'll start cleaning Judge Johnston's shirts and have them done before dinner."

Chapter 12

It was so comforting to see Momma smile again, and I just knew that things would begin to get better around here with the extra money coming in. After I got changed, that melody I had heard on a neighbor's radio kept going through my mind. I think it was called *Blue Skies.* It was a catchy little tune and one I really wanted to learn. But Momma was only interested in playing her hymns. I thought for a moment that since Momma was as happy as she was about the extra money coming in, maybe I could coax her into learning something different.

When I came back downstairs, Momma was still doing her sewing on the porch. So I snuck into the kitchen and pulled out a quarter from the laundry money jar and was going to put it to good use. I walked to the front of the house, and through the screen door I announced to Momma that I was going to take care of Judge Johnston's shirts right now.

"Okay, Lila, I might as well get dinner going for the two of us," she said.

I slipped out the back door and grabbed the wooden tub and filled it with water from the pump, and then got to washing the five shirts that Momma had picked up from the judge's home. Just as I finished and began to hang the shirts on the line, Momma called out: "Dinner's ready."

I finished hanging the shirts, dumped the dirty water out of the tub and placed it against the back of the house, then went to join her in the kitchen.

"So Momma, what's for dinner?" I asked.

"Lila, not too much, I'm afraid," she said. Just some grits with black-eyed peas and some corn bread I made. At least it will fill your stomach and you won't have to go to bed hungry like so many people in America do these days."

As we sat at the table, I asked Momma why she only ever wanted to play Christian hymns when there were so many pretty songs I had heard on the radio.

"Child, I was brought up on the Lord's hymns, and that's all I ever play. That fancy music you hear on the radio is for sinners," she said.

"But Momma, it couldn't hurt to learn something new once in a while."

"Well, maybe if it were a decent song. You know, Lila, one that offers hope for better days to come."

"Momma, I think I know just the song, and maybe I know where I can find the music for it," I said. "I'm going to run out for a while. I promise I'll be back in twenty minutes."

"Okay, Lila, but you be home before it gets dark. I'll take care of cleaning up the dinner dishes."

I kissed Momma on her cheek and said I would be back soon. I left the house and headed to Cobb Street where I knew there was a music store. I just had to get my hands on that song, *Blue Skies*, because I knew it would lift Momma's spirits even more, just as it did mine.

I finally reached the store and not a minute too soon, as they were getting ready to close for the day. I walked in and asked the man behind the counter if he had the sheet music for a song called *Blue Skies*? He pointed right behind me and there it was. I looked at the price, and it must have been my lucky day, because it would cost me only fifteen cents. I pulled a copy of the music and paid the man his money and promptly left the store.

As I was walking back to the house, I opened the sheet music and began learning the words to the song. Momma was a pretty good sight-reader, so I wanted to be ready to sing when she played it the first time. As I kept reading and walking, I bumped right into someone, and when I looked up, it was that darn young man again.

"Oh, I'm so sorry, Charles. My head seems to be somewhere else and I wasn't paying attention to where I was walking. It's funny how we keep running into each other."

"Yes, Lila, it *is* funny. Where are you headed, if you don't mind my asking?"

"I just picked up some new music for my Momma to learn on the piano, and I'm studying the words so I can sing along with her," I said.

Charles asked what the name of the song was, and I told him it was called *Blue Skies*. Once I said the name of the song, I noticed that the expression on Charles's face changed dramatically. It was almost as if he were angry, and yet sad at the same time.

"I really have to get going, Charles. Maybe we can talk another time," I said, before I hurried off.

As I headed back to the house, I wondered why Charles had grown so quiet. I guess it just wasn't for me to know, so I went on my way and tried to put it out of my mind.

Chapter 13

I was really hoping that Momma would like the song I had picked out. It was still oppressively hot by the time I returned home, and as I approached, I heard Momma warming up on the piano. When I walked into the parlor, there was none other than the Reverend Benson sitting in Momma's favorite chair.

"Good evening, Lila," the reverend said. "How have you been, Child?" he asked.

"I'm just fine, Reverend Benson. Even a blind hog can find an acorn now and then."

"Sounds like you might have had a bit of luck lately, Lila," the reverend said. Your mother has been telling me about your new position, and I wish you all the good luck in the world."

"Thank you, Reverend Benson. Yes, I got me a job at the Woolworth store, and right now, along with doing laundry for a few customers, life seems pretty good. Would you like something to drink, Reverend Benson?" I asked.

"Your mother has taken good care of me, Lila, but thank you for asking."

"Will you be staying long, Reverend Benson?" I asked.

"Actually, no. I have to get a move on—just wanted to stop by and talk to your mother about some of the hymns I would like to hear at next Sunday's service. And now I guess

I'd better get going. It's getting late."

Momma got up from the piano and walked Reverend Benson to the front door. After he left she returned to the parlor and asked: "Did you find that special song you were looking for, Lila?"

"Yes, I sure did Momma. It's called *Blue Skies,* and I think you're going to like it."

Well, Lila, let's see what you have," Momma said.

I placed the sheet music in front of Momma, and as she began to play, I started to sing along. After we had practiced it a couple of times, I asked what she thought of it.

"You know, Lila, I guess you can teach an old dog a new trick every now and then. This is a beautiful song and the words ring so true in offering hope for better days coming.

"Let's try it one more time, Momma, and maybe just pick up the tempo a little bit."

Momma looked at me and laughed, which is something I hadn't seen her do in a long time. As she began to play, I began to sing as loud as I could, because I had a feeling that Charles might be standing outside, and sure enough, as I looked out across the street, there he was. I had almost finished the song before I took another look, but by then Charles was gone. I wondered again why the name of that song seemed to cause him the vapors. Maybe someday I just might find out.

Chapter 14

After Momma and I had some fun with her playing and my singing, we decided to make it an early night. In the morning Momma would deliver Judge Johnston's shirts, and I had to be at work by eight a.m. I knew the country was in bad shape and everyone was hoping that President Roosevelt would keep his promise in getting America back to work. At least I was going to do my part, and with this new job, I just knew that better days were ahead, exactly like the words to *Blue Skies* said. I turned down the lamp and then blew out the flame and fell off to sleep.

The morning came soon enough and I got dressed in record time. I went downstairs and saw that Momma already had the kettle on the wood stove, so I knew my cup of coffee was would be ready in no time.

"Momma, after you drop off the judge's shirts, what were you planning on doing?" I asked.

"I think I'll take some of the money from the laundry jar and do a little food shopping, Lila. I may even just stop by your store, if you don't mind."

"Oh please, Momma, don't do that on my first day. I'm going to be nervous enough as it is."

Momma laughed, which was something she didn't do often, and said, "Don't worry, then, Lila. I won't stop by today. But maybe someday I just might. I have plenty enough to keep me busy today, and I may just stop by the bakery to see if Mr. Crawford might have anything he needs cleaned.

"Oh thank you, Momma," I said. "That certainly would help me out. I really don't want to let him down now that we have his business."

I gave Momma a kiss and told her I would see her after five p.m. when my shift ended. I went on my way, humming the new song that I had purchased for Momma to play, and just couldn't get that tune out of my head. As I approached the store, Horace was standing outside, fussing with a chalkboard sign, writing on it the specials of the day so customers could see what was on sale that day.

"Good morning, Horace," I said.

"You're right on time, Lila. You see that lady over there in the white blouse? he asked."

"Yes, Horace, I see her."

"That's Mrs. Wallingford, and she'll show you how to work the register. It's not difficult, and there's a stool right by the register, so you can make yourself comfortable."

"Thank you, Horace," I said, as I walked over to Mrs. Wallingford.

"Good morning, Mrs. Wallingford. My name is *Lila,* and Horace sent me to see you so you can show me how to work the register."

"It's a pleasure meeting you, Lila. The register isn't difficult at all. When customers are finished with their meal, the waitress will give them their check and then they will walk over to the register to pay. Whatever figure is written at the bottom of the check is what the customer owes. So if you had a check that said *$1.00,* all you have to do is press the key that has the one dollar sign on it, and then just turn this crank on the side of the register all the way around and the cash draw will open, so you can collect the money and make change if you have to."

"Well, that seems pretty easy, Mrs. Wallingford and it looks like I have my first customer already," I said.

Mrs. Wallingford stood to the left side of me to watch. The customer was an older man that had come in for a cup of coffee and a doughnut. I took the check he handed me and saw the cost was eight cents. The man handed me a dime, so I pressed the button that said zero and eight and then turned the crank on the side of the register. With one turn, the cash draw opened, along with the sound of a small bell. After taking the dime from the gentleman, I gave him back two cents and then closed the draw to the register.

"Have a wonderful day, young lady," the man said.

"You too, Sir," I responded.

Lila, you did that flawlessly." Mrs. Wallingford said. "You're a fast learner, Lila, and I think you'll do just fine."

"Why thank you, Mrs. Wallingford. I'll do my best."

As the day wore on, business began to pick up as we got closer to lunchtime. One thing I didn't realize was that I would get a free sandwich for lunch, as well as fifteen minutes of free time to eat.

Olivia, the waitress, was a really nice lady, who took me on a quick trip back to the kitchen to meet Oscar, the cook. I couldn't believe the amount of food Oscar was able to prepare in such a short time; he obviously was a pro. I learned that both Olivia and Oscar had been with the store for years. After that, when things weren't busy, Olivia would come over and we just talked about anything and everything under the sun. In time, we became pretty good friends.

My first day on the job went quickly, and before I knew it, the clock in the store said five p.m., and it was time for me to leave. I had to walk to the time clock just outside the manager's office to punch in the time of when I arrived and when I left. So after I punched out, my first day at my first official job was now complete.

As I was walking back to the front of the store to leave, Horace stopped me, and with a broad smile on his face, told me: "Lila, you were magnificent today. I'll see you bright and early tomorrow morning."

"Thank you Horace, I'll be here."

Chapter 15

As I left the store I realized how tired a person could become just sitting around and collecting money from people after they finished their meals. But at least this part of the day was over. On my way back home I wondered what Momma might have for dinner, but of greater concern was whether Momma had brought back any additional laundry that had to be taken care of. When I finally had made it home, something going on in the kitchen smelled awfully good.

"Momma, where are you?" I called.

"I'm out back. Be right there, Lila."

I looked out the back door and sure enough, Momma had stopped at the bakery and there was a ton of washing to do. Momma was drying her hands before she came back into the kitchen, and said she had taken care of the majority of the wash from the bakery.

"So Lila, how did your first day go at the store?" Momma asked.

"Momma, it wasn't hard at all, and I was surprised that the job even includes a free lunch. I had a tuna sandwich with those fancy potato chips, and even a pickle and a coke. Horace said I was magnificent, and told me to be back bright and early tomorrow morning. I really enjoy getting out and talking to people, Momma."

"Just don't forget about those two girls that were

murdered, Child. You just can't tell these days much about people, especially people not from around these parts," Momma cautioned.

"I know, Momma. You don't have to keep reminding me. But what in the world smells so good?"

"Lila, it was going to be a surprise, but I used some of the additional laundry money and did a little food shopping. What you smell, Child, is the best home-baked sweet potato pie you have ever had. I also stopped at the butcher and bought us some chop meat for a meat loaf. Tonight, Girl, we are celebrating!"

"Momma, that sounds so wonderful. I just hope I can keep my eyes open long enough to eat it all. Lord, I am so tired."

"Well, as tired as you may be, you still have work to do. I stopped at the bakery and Mr. Crawford had another load to be taken care of. I've finished most of it. Think I have just a few towels left to go."

"Momma, I can do them right now. I'll get everything hung up to dry while you finish in the kitchen."

"Why thank you, Lila," Momma said. "Dinner will be ready in about fifteen minutes. Now go scoot and get those towels done."

I headed out the back to finish up the laundry, when all of a sudden I had that strange feeling again, that someone was staring at me. I looked around real good, but didn't see a living soul. I thought I must have been over-tired from all the excitement of the day, so I just tried to forget about it. I got to work and finished up the towels and got everything hung on the clothesline just as Momma called me for dinner.

"Momma, I can't remember the last time we ate this

good."

"Been a long time, Child. But the good lord provides when he sees fit to help those that help themselves," she said.

"Well, Momma, after a meal like this, I'll sing like a canary tonight. Can we do that new song again, *Blue Skies*?"

"Of course we can, Lila. You know I took a few minutes to read the words to that song, and it sure makes me feel good about a better tomorrow. Things just have to start turning around for us."

Chapter 16

After dinner was finished, I helped momma clean the dishes, along with the pots and pans, and then we retired to the parlor.

"You know, Momma, with the extra money that's coming in, maybe we can get the piano tuned one day."

"Lila, I don't know," Momma said. "I was talking to Judge Johnston's wife when I picked up his shirts, and she told me that the man who tunes their piano charges them a whole dollar to tune it. That might be a little too steep for us."

"Well, Momma, we don't have to do it right away. Maybe we can afford it after a few weeks with the money from my job."

"We'll see, Lila. I just don't want us to be going too crazy spending what we don't have in hand yet," Momma replied.

As usual, Momma started off with a hymn, and after singing several hymns, I told momma I was really tired. "Momma, I'm so full I can hardly keep my eyes open. Let's do the new song and call it a night."

"Okay Lila, here's your introduction."

Momma played the introduction to *Blue Skies* and then I jumped in. About half way through the song I began just walking around the parlor when I happened to look out the window and saw Charles standing across the street. As I got into the second verse of the song, I noticed he had what appeared to be a stick or part of a branch in his hand. All of a sudden, he just took that piece of wood and snapped it right in half with both hands.

By the time the song ended I had walked back over to the piano, and when I turned to look out the window once more, Charles was gone. I thanked Momma for playing my song again, and decided I would retire for the night—I just couldn't keep my eyes open any longer. I gave Momma a kiss and told her I would be up bright and early in the morning and would be happy to drop off Mr. Crawford's laundry on my way to work.

As I walked upstairs to get changed into my bedclothes, I kept wondering what it was about that song that seemed to make Charles angry enough to break that stick he had. But honestly, I was so tired I really didn't care at that point, and just wanted to get to sleep.

The sun was just coming up the next morning when a neighbor's roosters began crowing their heads off at the first signs of daylight. I thought I'd better get myself together, because I needed the extra time to drop off Mr. Crawford's laundry. I sure didn't want to be late getting to my new full-time job at the Five and Dime.

After I got dressed I went downstairs, only to find a note Momma had left on the table. She had taken all the laundry and would deliver it herself to Mr. Crawford's bakery shop. Bless her big old southern heart! Land sakes, that woman was always full of surprises. The kettle was still hot on the stove, so I made myself a cup of coffee, and found one other surprise Momma had left for me. A warm slice of her sweet potato pie, and that was all I needed to get my day started.

I cleaned up after breakfast and left the house to walk down to the store. It was seven forty-five, and I was only one street away. I turned the corner and then stopped dead in my tracks when I saw Charles, leaning next to a building.

"Good day, Charles," I said.

"Good day to you, Lila. Are you off to work this morning?"

"Why, yes I am, and I'd better get going or I'm going to be late; I don't want any trouble with my new job. Maybe we can talk another time, Charles."

As I began to walk away, Charles said, "I wish you would never sing that damned song again."

Charles's voice seemed angry, but I paid him no mind, and pretended I didn't even hear what he had said; but I swear, when he said that to me those chills and goose bumps were all over my arms, and all I wanted to do was get into the store as soon as I could.

As I walked into the store, Horace gave me a great big smile and asked if I was ready for another exciting day.

I smiled back and said to Horace, "It's only seven fifty-eight, and my day has been exciting enough already, Horace. Oh look, we already have customers coming in. I better get behind the counter right quick."

Chapter 17

It was only my second day on the job, but I recognized some of the same customers that I had seen the day before, and thought they must make a routine stop in the morning for coffee and maybe something to eat. Olivia was busy taking orders for Oscar in the kitchen, and it sure seemed like a lot of people were shopping today. The cash register faced the front of the store, and while I was waiting for customers to check out before getting on their way, I just loved watching people go about their business as they walked by on the street outside. At that moment, I noticed Charles looking in the window. and then I could tell that he spotted me as I sat behind the register. I had no idea why he seemed upset about my singing *Blue Skies*, but before this day was out, I wanted to get an answer.

After my first customer paid his bill and was on his way, I noticed that Charles had disappeared again. I thought to myself, *How is it that this man can just disappear in the blink of an eye?* I just couldn't be bothered with it at the moment, with so many people in the store, so I just went about my business and did the job Horace was paying me for.

Lunchtime came soon enough, and Oscar had made me a big bologna sandwich with mustard, along with one of those really sour pickles that I just loved. Olivia took over the register while I ate in the back of the store. After I finished up lunch and went back to relieve Olivia, the place was so busy that even Horace was helping to get dishes off the counter so they could be cleaned. I couldn't believe the number of people that were in the store, and I asked Horace if he was having some kind of sale today."

"No. Lila. I guess people just wait until the last minute before spending money on something that they really need. But it sure seems like today is going to be a big day for the store," he said.

I must have checked out at least ten people when I heard a commotion at the far end of the counter. It was Horace, talking loudly to a man I couldn't see, with all the customers that were seated at the counter. But it sure was raising a fuss as people turned to hear what all the trouble was about. The next thing I saw just shocked me. It was Charles, whom I hadn't noticed come in, having a cup of coffee and a doughnut. The next thing I knew Horace, a pretty big man, took Charles by his collar and escorted him out of the store.

I heard him say to Charles: "We don't want any freeloaders in this establishment. If you can't pay, then you have no business being here. Get on your way, or I'll call the police."

As Horace walked back into the store, I stopped him and asked what had happened.

"Lila, I know times are tough, but if I let one person try to get food without paying for it, others will come in right behind that man, and I can't have that. We're not a soup kitchen."

Horace then walked back to his office and picked up the phone on his desk, but I was too far away to hear who he was talking to. The rest of the day was quite busy but pretty uneventful, so when five o'clock came, I just went to the time clock and punched out. I said goodnight to Horace, Oscar, and Olivia, and started on my way back home.

As I was walking home, I thought I might possibly see Charles on the street, since he always seemed to show up when you least expected him. But this time Charles was nowhere to be found. I thought after what had happened in the store today that maybe he had just decided to move on to another city or town, like so many drifters that passed through. When I eventually made it back to the house, I found Momma out back doing more laundry. I walked out and asked her how her day had gone?

"Oh, hi there, Lila. I didn't even hear you. How did your day go at the store?" she asked.

I didn't dare say anything to Momma about what had happened, so I just told her it was a busy day, but nothing unusual to speak about.

"Well, I'll be done here shortly and then we can have dinner. Why don't you go inside and get cleaned up. I'll be in soon."

I went back into the house to change, but first I decided to walk into the parlor to look out the front window to see if Charles might be around, but there was no sign of him. I sat at Momma's piano and opened the sheet music to *Blue Skies*. I wasn't sure why this song seemed to upset Charles as it did, but it was such a pretty and hopeful song, and I wasn't going to let some stranger stop me from singing it. After all, he didn't have to stand across the street and listen.

Chapter 18

After Momma and I finished dinner, we retired to the parlor as we always did. As Momma began to warm up and stretch her fingers, I walked over to the window to see if Charles might be around, but there wasn't any sign of him. As Momma began to play her first hymn, she asked if I was ready, and we ended up getting through five of Momma's favorite songs. Then she turned to me and said, "You ready, Lila, to sing *Blue Skies*?"

"Sure, Momma," I said. "Let's do it."

Momma began to play, and just as I finished singing the first chorus, a rock suddenly came crashing through the parlor window, breaking the glass into a million little pieces. Momma was startled and asked, "What in the Sam Hill just happened?"

Momma, it looks like someone threw a rock through our window. I can't imagine why someone would do that to us."

Momma got up from the piano as I went to fetch the broom and dust pan so I could sweep up the shards of glass that had fallen on the floor. When I returned, I looked out the window again, but no one was on the street. It was a little hard to see at night because the city of Atlanta hadn't brought streetlights to our neighborhood yet. That was supposed to be done when President Roosevelt got his work programs going, and hopefully that wouldn't be much longer.

After Momma and I got the glass cleaned up, she went upstairs and grabbed a sheet and came back and hung it over the broken window. The last thing we needed was having a house full of flies and other bugs coming in.

"I declare, Lila, I can't imagine why anyone would do such a thing. You know it's going to cost us a lot of money to get that window fixed," Momma said.

"Don't worry, Momma. If I have to work harder, I will, and we'll get it fixed. Why don't you find out tomorrow how much the repair will cost, and we can figure out how long it will take us to save enough to fix it."

About that time Momma just sat down in her favorite chair and began to sob. "We have tried so hard to make ends meet, and just when you think life is beginning to turn around, another expense we didn't need hits us like a train wreck."

"I know, Momma. It's going to set us back a bit, but we'll get through this, and whoever did this will get theirs in time," I said. "Don't cry, Momma; just remember the words to that song: *blue days, all of them gone, nothin' but blue skies from now on.*"

Momma grabbed hold of my hand and said, "Lila, I don't know what I would do without your presence in this house. I had all but given up on ever getting ahead, but I know this too shall pass, and the righteous hearts in this world will have better days ahead."

"Amen to that, Momma," I said. "Why don't you go up and lie down. I'll take care of things down here and I'll blow out the lamps for the night."

"Thank you, Child. I really don't know what I would do without you."

After Momma went upstairs, I looked outside one more time to see if Charles might have been around, but I didn't see a soul. So I locked the front and back doors, as I always did, and started up the stairs to my room. I just couldn't understand why someone would be so mean as to throw a rock through our window.

As I tried to fall asleep, I felt troubled right down to my soul that some person had a reason do such a thing. I knew the expense of the repair would set us back. But we were strong people and I kept reminding myself, like the song said, that there would be *nothin' but blue skies from now on.*

Chapter 19

The night was uneventful, or at least that's what I thought until I came downstairs. Momma was fidgeting like a pregnant hen and barely said a word.

"Are you okay, Momma?" I asked.

"Lila, someone must have been in the house last night, and I'm afraid for both of us with so many lonely and hungry men roaming the streets these days."

"Why? What ever has happened, Momma?" I asked. Momma got up from the kitchen table and walked me into the parlor. The sheet we had hung over the broken window had been torn down, and when I looked at the piano, all the music that Momma had placed on the piano was still there, except for one, which was ripped to shreds—the music to *Blue Skies.* Whoever did this must have been very angry, because the music was torn into little pieces and thrown all over the floor. But the worst part was knowing that some stranger had been in our house without our even knowing it.

Momma was fit to be tied when she announced: "I'm going over to talk to Judge Johnston and see if there is anything we should do."

"Momma, why talk to him? Maybe we should just go over to a neighbor's house that has a phone and call the police."

"Lila, don't you worry about a thing, and just let me handle it. Now go on; get yourself off to work and don't be late."

I went back into the kitchen to get a cup of coffee. I still was so upset that someone had been in our home and we didn't even know it until this morning. Then I thought about the murder of those two girls in Bucks County. I just never could figure out why good things seemed to happen in our lives, and then out of the blue, something bad followed. I found a left-over biscuit to eat for my breakfast, then I got my thoughts together and gave Momma a kiss and told her I would see her for dinner.

I left the house at 7:30 and noticed a couple of neighbors outside sweeping their sidewalks, as if nothing at all out of the ordinary had happened. In fact, on my way to the store nothing seemed unusual other than the fact that I didn't see Charles anywhere around that morning.

Horace greeted me as I arrived at the store just in the nick of time. After I punched in on my time card, I said good morning to Olivia and Oscar, and then took my place behind the register. Just as the day before, the morning crowd piled in for breakfast, and my day had begun.

I knew the lunch crowd would be in before long and sure enough, like clockwork, the store began to get crowded. I loved watching people, and there was one young man in particular that kind of caught my eye. He must have been in his early twenties, and was very well dressed. As customers came over to me to pay their checks, I thought perhaps I would be able to start a conversation with him when he was ready to pay.

Now was the moment. The young man was just about finished as I saw him wipe his mouth with his napkin, and take one last sip of his drink. He looked at his watch, picked up his check, pulled out some pocket change to leave as a tip for Olivia, and began to walk toward me.

"Good afternoon, Miss," he said to me, as he handed me his check.

Now was my chance, so I smiled and replied, "Good afternoon, Sir." Then I felt myself blush as I added, "You are one of the best-dressed men I have seen in here for a while."

He grinned and extended his hand and said, "Why, thank you, uh, um—I don't even know your name. My name is *Peter Johnston*. I work at the bank across the street."

I must have turned all colors of the rainbow and my face must have lit up like a lighthouse as I said to him, "Well, hello, Peter. It's a pleasure to meet such a handsome young man. My name is *Lila. Lila Hartley*."

"Well, Miss Lila, you sure are easy on the eyes," he said, as he smiled broadly.

"Why, thank you Peter, that is the sweetest thing I've heard all day," I replied.

Peter then asked if I had been working here long, and I told him I had just started this week.

He glanced at his watch again, and then said, "Geez, it's getting late, and I have to get back to the bank. This might seem like I'm being a bit forward, Lila, but would you be interested in taking in a picture show with me some time?"

"Why, Peter, I think I would take kindly to that invitation," I said.

"I'll tell you what, Lila, I'll be back in tomorrow and we'll make it official, as long as your parents won't mind."

"Peter, that won't be a problem. It's just me and my Momma, and I think she might actually feel a little better knowing that I was going out with a successful young banker. She's been all upset that the police haven't caught the person that murdered those two girls over in Bucks County."

"I know," he replied. "Terrible thing when people can't even be safe in their own homes these days. Well, I'd better get back to work, Lila. I'll see you tomorrow at lunchtime."

I was so flustered that I even forgot to give Peter his change, but I knew I would see him the next day and could give it to him then.

Chapter 20

It was getting close to quitting time when Olivia walked over to me and said, "You seem to have had an exciting day, Lila."

"How so?" I asked.

"Oh, you can't fool me, Lila. I know when a young man is interested in a pretty young thing like you. Why, look at you blush, Young Lady. I think he thinks you're really cute."

"Oh stop, Olivia. He just wanted to talk a bit, but then he did ask me out to go see a picture show."

"Well Darlin', I do hope you said *yes*. He's really a dashing-looking young man."

"He said he would be in tomorrow, so we'll see if he even remembers me, Olivia. Listen, I have to get going, as I'm sure Momma has some laundry waiting for me to get done, so I'd better get a move on."

"You take care, Lila. See you in the morning," Olivia said.

As I walked out of the store I looked around and the streets this time of day didn't seem too busy. As I began walking to the house, I had that strange feeling again that someone was watching me. I stopped in my tracks and looked around, but didn't see anyone. I guess I was just being a bit nervous after what happened last night at the house. But I did think it was strange that I hadn't seen Charles anywhere around all day.

When I reached the house, Momma was in the kitchen

heating up some of the meat loaf we had the night before, along with a pot of rice and some black-eyed peas.

"Oh Lila, land sakes, I didn't even hear you come in the house. How was your day?"

"Why, Momma? There wasn't anything special, except one thing."

"What's that?" Momma asked.

"Well, at lunch time there was this dashing young man who was very well dressed, and after he finished his lunch and came over to pay his bill, he introduced himself to me."

"Really!" Momma exclaimed.

"Yes, Momma. He really seemed like one of those movie star dreamboats you always read about in those Hollywood magazines."

"Lila, does this young man have a name?" Momma asked.

"Why, of course he does. His name is Peter Johnston, and he works at the bank across the street from the store."

"Hmm," Momma said. "I wonder?"

"You wonder what, momma?"

"I can't be sure, but just maybe that young man is the son of Judge Johnston, whose shirts we wash."

"Do you think so, Momma?" I asked.

"It is possible, though the Johnstons do have a pretty big family in these parts. I guess you'll find out soon enough."

Momma, I hope you don't mind, but he asked me to go with him to the picture show one night. It's only for one night, and I promise I'll be back at a decent hour."

"Lilia," Momma said, "you're a beautiful young lady and I know you've stayed around this old house longer than you should have. But you know, when the time is right, my little song bird will spread those wings and live a life of her own."

"Oh Momma, thank you so much for understanding. I wasn't sure if you might be upset or something."

"Lila, you go and get cleaned up and we'll have a nice dinner in a little while."

"Thanks, Momma, I'll be right back."

After I washed up, I asked Momma if there was any laundry to be taken care of.

"Yes, Lila. I have several shirts of the Judge's, as well as some from Dr. Matthews that they will need tomorrow."

"Momma, I'll get to them right after dinner. I promise."

After dinner was finished and the dishes were washed and put away, I told Momma I would be out back taking care of those shirts for the judge and the doctor.

"Now, Lila, don't get them shirts mixed up or we're going to have a real mess on our hands."

"Don't worry, Momma, I won't get them mixed up," I said.

I walked out to the back of the house and took the wash tub and began to fill it with water. While I was waiting, I had that strange feeling again. I looked around the yard and the woods nearby and didn't see anyone. But as sure as day turns to night, I knew someone was watching me, and that someone had to be Charles.

I separated the two bundles of shirts and took care of both of them pretty fast and began to hang them up to dry. Then, out of the corner of my eye, I thought I saw something move over in the woods. It could have been an animal, or maybe a person. At that point, all I wanted to do was dump the water out of the tub and just get back into the house.

When I came back inside, Momma was already warming

up at the piano, but before we got to singing, I asked Momma if she had found out how much the window would cost to get fixed?

"I did speak to Mr. Enright at the glass store, and he said he would come over tomorrow and measure what he needed, and then he could give me a price."

"I sure hope it won't cost us an arm and a leg, Momma," I said.

As Momma began to play her hymns, I walked over to the broken window and peeked out behind the sheet we had put up, and sure enough, there was Charles, walking back and forth with a stick, as he ran it across a picket fence. It was making that kind of sound that a bicycle makes when some of the kids use clothespins to attach baseball cards on the spokes so they go *clickety-clack* as they ride their bikes up and down the streets.

I stepped back from the window and started to sing to Momma's hymns she was playing. We did this for about ten minutes and then Momma said she was tired.

"Momma, can we just do one more song? You know which one I mean."

"You're lucky, Young Lady. I have a good memory, and I already know it by heart. Do you remember all the words, Lila?" she asked.

"Yes, I sure do, Momma."

As Momma played the introduction, I walked back over to the window to take another look at Charles, and as soon as he heard that song playing, he again snapped that stick in half, and gave me the coldest and hardest stare I had ever seen.

I walked over to the piano as Momma was finishing, and

asked her to look out the broken window to see if anyone might have been listening to us. Momma got up from the piano and said, “Lila, there isn't a soul on the street that I can see. Why did you want me to look, Child?”

“Oh, I just thought we might have a secret admirer, that's all.”

Chapter 21

I couldn't worry myself silly about what was bothering Charles every time he heard that song, and it was getting late. I had to be up early and get to work on time, so I just got ready for bed and prayed that there wouldn't be any other problems during the night like we had the night before.

The next morning, as I got dressed, I thought to myself that the night seemed to have passed without another strange incident. When I got downstairs, I asked Momma if she had noticed anything this morning when she got up.

"No, Lila, everything seems to be in its place. Why don't you just go look out back and check for me," Momma said.

I walked to the back of the house and when I opened the door I couldn't believe my eyes. Every shirt hanging on the clothesline had been torn to shreds. I screamed, calling for Momma, and when she saw what had happened she just broke down in tears.

"How will I ever replace those expensive shirts?" Momma asked. "The judge and the doctor will never give me their business again. I just can't believe someone would do this. Someone surely must have a sick mind."

"Momma, you have to get in touch with the police. First the window, and now this. It has to stop, Momma!"

"Lila, don't you worry about me. I'll take care of this after I talk to the judge and Doc Matthews. You'd better get yourself off to your job, or we may lose that income as well."

I kissed Momma and told her not to fret, and that I would see her after I finished work at the store. I knew I was leaving Momma in a state, but I had to get to work and it was already getting late. I took off as fast as I could and never did see hide nor hair of Charles all the way to work, and made it to the store just in the nick of time. I was nearly out of breath when I punched in, and Horace asked me if everything was all right.

"Oh, Horace, my momma and I have been having a devil of a time these last two days. First someone threw a rock through our front window last night, and this morning when we went out to remove the laundry that Momma had done for Judge Johnston and Dr. Matthews, we found the shirts all torn to pieces. I just can't imagine who would do such a thing."

"Horace looked concerned and said, "Maybe the rock was thrown by some kids, but I can't figure out why anyone would tear up someone's laundry. I hope your mother calls the police."

"I sure hope she does too, Horace. I'm getting a little nervous, now that this has happened two days in a row."

The regular morning customers were arriving, and as I watched the clock on the wall, I couldn't wait for Peter to show up for lunch. He was such a handsome young man, tall with jet black hair and a cute little dimple right in the center of his chin.

When the lunch crowd began to show up, I watched every person that came in to eat, but it was now past one p.m. and I still hadn't seen Peter. My heart was sinking, and then, like a bolt out of the blue, I saw him walking across the street to the store.

Chapter 22

Peter walked right up to me and said, "Hi, Lila. I know I'm a little late today, but the strangest thing happened to me just a little while ago."

"Strange in what way, Peter?" I asked.

"Well, I was getting ready to come over for lunch when my phone rang. It was my father, who said that the woman who does his laundry had come over to the house to deliver his shirts, only to explain that someone had torn them all to shreds. The woman was extremely upset and was beside herself, and he tried to console her as best he could."

As Peter was telling me the story, my heart sank, as I suddenly remembered what Momma had said about the possibility that Peter was Judge Johnston's son.

"Peter, can I ask you a question?"

"Sure, Lila, what is it?"

"Peter, is your father Judge Johnston?"

"Why, yes Lila. How did you know that?" he asked.

"Peter, the reason I know is because it is my mother who has been doing the judge's laundry for years, and I just now realized the judge must be your father. Mamma was heartbroken this morning when she saw what had happened to his shirts. And it wasn't only your father's shirts—whoever did this did the same thing to Dr. Matthew's shirts. Not only that, but someone had thrown a rock and broke our front window the night before, but now with these shirts that were destroyed, I'm really worried, Peter. And I am so sorry about your father's shirts."

"Lila, you mean to tell me that it's your mother that has been doing our laundry all these years? Well now, ain't that something. It truly is a small world, Lila. But don't you worry about the shirts. My father told me he called the police, and then drove your mother back to her house so they could take a look around. And on top of that, Dad said he not only paid your mother for doing the laundry, but also gave her a ten-dollar bill that would go toward fixing the window, and even made arrangements to get a man to go to the house today to get it done."

I felt the tears welling up in my eyes as Peter took my hand and said, "Don't you cry, Lila. Everything is going to be all right, and the best part is that you and I are going to the picture show tonight. It will be just you and me, Lila."

"Do you really mean that, Peter?" I asked.

"I sure do, Lila. Just write your address down to give to me after I finish lunch, and I'll pick you up in my car at seven tonight. Have we got a deal, Miss Lila?"

"Peter, you are just too kind, and you have such a wonderful smile. I'll be ready for you at seven tonight. Now you'd better get something to eat."

As Peter sat at the counter eating, I scribbled down my address to give to him when he was finished. Somehow I just never made the connection yesterday when Peter mentioned his last name, and I wanted to thank him again for what his father had done for Momma. This day was turning out better than I ever thought possible.

After Peter had finished eating, he came over to the

register to pay his bill, and asked, “Do you have that address ready for me, Lila?”

“Yes, Peter, here it is, and I’ll be ready right on time,” I replied.

“Great, Lila, I'll see you then. But first, I'm going to go over to Mr. Jessie's clothing store and pick up some new shirts for my dad. His birthday is coming up in three more days, and now at least I know what I can get him. I even know his size. So I’d better get going now. See you at seven sharp.”

After Peter paid his bill, I just watched him walk across the street to the bank. I felt like some moon-struck fan that drools when he listens to Bing Crosby crooning.

Chapter 23

I felt so much better now for Momma, especially after leaving her in such a wreck this morning. Not only would Peter replace the shirts for his father, but Judge Johnston had contacted the police and even helped Momma in paying for a new window. I couldn't wait to get home and tell her about Peter and what a small world it really was.

When the clock hit five, I punched out, and Horace cautioned me to be careful on the way home.

“I will, Horace. But if I have to, I can run like the wind,” I said.

“You just be mindful of people around you, Lila. With all these panhandlers coming into town from up north, you just never know these days.”

I said goodnight to Olivia and Oscar and made my way home just as fast as I could. Even if Charles was lurking around in the shadows, I would just ignore him and head on my way. I couldn't wait to see Momma again.

When I finally reached the house, Momma was standing outside with the man that had already repaired our window. I walked up to them just as Momma asked for the bill.

“It's already taken care of, Mam,” the man told her.

Momma and I were shocked that someone would do that for us. But Momma had stopped off somewhere and gotten change for the ten dollar bill Judge Johnston had given her, and gave the man a two-dollar tip for his troubles. He thanked her, tipped his hat, got into his truck and drove away.

"Momma, the new window looks good, but you'll never guess what happened to me today," I blurted out.

Momma looked a bit amused and said, "Let's go inside and have something to eat, Lila. I already have dinner ready, and you can tell me all about it as we eat."

As we sat down for dinner we said *grace* first, as we always did, and then I found myself talking a mile a minute.

"Slow down, Child, or you're going to have a stroke. Now what's all this you wanted to tell me?"

"Momma, that young man, Peter, really is the judge's son, and he asked me if I wanted to go to a picture show with him tonight. It's okay, isn't it, Momma?" I asked.

"Of course it is, Lila. What time will he be here?"

"He said seven sharp, Momma, and that only gives me an hour to get ready."

Momma took my hand and said, "Lila, with everything that has happened around here in the last couple of days, I'm so happy for you. Now scoot and go get ready, and if you want help braiding your hair, just let me know."

I ran upstairs and got into my Sunday church dress with the yellow roses, and then ran back downstairs to ask Momma if she could braid my hair on both sides. I just wanted a little something to make me look kind of special. What that woman could do with hair and a few bobby pins was truly a sight to behold.

Before I knew it, I heard a horn blow twice, and no sooner did I get to the front door than I saw Peter standing there with a bouquet of flowers.

As I opened the door and greeted Peter, I remarked at how beautiful the flowers were. At that moment, Momma walked to the front door and greeted Peter as well, while I fetched a vase from the parlor to place the flowers in. By the time I had gotten back to Momma and Peter, he was telling her that his father made sure the police would be around our neighborhood, so that if there was any more trouble they would take care of it.

"Peter, please thank your father for everything he has done for us, and for his kindness and understanding.

"I certainly will," Peter replied.

Before we left the house, Momma gave me the eight dollars that was left over from the judge's money he gave her for repairing the window and said, "I want you to return this to the judge and thank him for what he did."

"I will, Momma," I said.

As we were leaving the house, Momma waved to us, and at that moment there was a clap of thunder and the skies opened up. Peter and I ran for the car, and he even opened the car door for me. As he ran around to the driver's side to get in, I noticed that he had brought along an umbrella that he had left in his car.

"My oh my, Peter. This is one fancy car you have," I said.

Peter told me it was a graduation present after he finished college.

"Just what kind of car is it, Peter?" I asked.

"Lila, this is a brand new 1933 Packard. Pretty nifty huh?"

"I'd say, Peter. It's a beauty. But we have to do one thing before we go, and Momma insists I do this."

"What's that, Lila?" Peter asked.

"Peter, your dad gave Momma a ten-dollar bill toward having our window fixed, but I guess your dad had already made arrangements to have it taken care of. Momma got change for the ten and gave the repairman a two-dollar tip, and she insists that I return the eight dollars left back to your father in person. I hope you won't mind our going out of the way so I can do that."

"Lila, it's no problem at all, and I think Dad will appreciate your mother's wanting to return the funds that were left over. Boy, it's really pouring cats and dogs. We'd better get going, or we'll miss the movie."

Peter started the engine and off we went.

Chapter 24

Once we got going I asked Peter how far out of the way his parents' home would be, and he said it was only about a mile once we crossed the railroad tracks that ran just behind my home. I had a pretty good idea where Peter was going. That section of town outside the city of Atlanta was where all the large homes and estates were located, and I could only imagine the type of home he lived in.

It took only seven minutes to get to the house, and I was stunned as we pulled into a large circular driveway with a fountain in the center. The house was huge, with beautiful stonework and more windows than I could even begin to count. It was pouring, and Peter said he would get the umbrella and walk me to the front door.

"Peter," I said, "that won't be necessary. You're already soaking wet—you'll catch your death of cold. Just give me the umbrella and I'll take care of it."

Peter asked if I was sure I wanted to do this, and I said, "Of course I do, Silly. I can handle this, Peter."

I grabbed the umbrella and opened car door, ran to the front door and rang the bell. Within a moment, the front door opened and a very large Negro servant dressed in what looked like a black tuxedo asked if he could help me.

I asked if Judge Johnston was available, and the servant replied: "He is in his bath, Miss. Can I be of assistance?"

He noticed Peter's car in the driveway, otherwise he probably would have sent me on my way.

"Could you please do me a favor and give these eight dollars to Judge Johnston and tell him I said to thank him for the repair to Mrs. Hartley's window."

The servant looked confused, but said he would do as I wished. "Is there anything else I may do for you, Madam?"

The look on my face must have amused him, as I had never been called *madam* in my life. So I just said, "Thank you. He'll understand what the money is for."

"Very well, Madam. I'll make sure he gets it," he said.

I returned to the car, closed the umbrella, jumped inside and closed the car door. I asked Peter who that manservant was.

"Oh, that's Steven. He's my father's major-domo."

"A major *what*?" I asked."

Peter laughed and said, "He's my father's head butler. We have several servants, and Steven pretty much runs the house for the family."

"My goodness, Peter. I guess being a judge has its benefits. I never thought that houses were this big."

"Lila, there are some a lot larger than this around Atlanta," Peter said.

I know a strange look came over my face then, because Peter asked if there was something wrong.

"Wrong? What could be wrong, Peter? You live in a gorgeous mansion, and I live on the other side of the tracks in a house that's ready to fall apart. We don't have electric and it's drafty and cold in the winter. I just feel so out of place."

"Lila, don't let the size of the house impress you. I know that the depression has taken a great toll on our country, but things will get better now that we have President Roosevelt in the White House. I just have a feeling that things will start to turn around for everyone. Don't concern yourself with what others have. You're still my *Georgia peach*, and we're going to have a great time this evening. Hopefully by the time the movie ends, even the skies will clear."

"Is that a promise, Peter?"

"I promise, Lila," Peter declared.

Peter took out a handkerchief and wiped away the rainwater that was dripping down my face.

"Peter Johnston, you are truly a southern gentleman."

Peter then placed the car in gear and within a few minutes we were at the movie theater. The rain had nearly stopped and that was good, but the parking lot was full.

"I shouldn't do this," Peter said, "but I'm going to back the car into that dark alley just far enough to get it off the street. If I get a ticket, my dad will kill me."

We both had a good laugh over that. The alley was right next to the theater, so we didn't have to walk all that far. Peter walked up to the window at the theater and bought two tickets for the show.

"Peter, I don't even know what we're going to see," I admitted, when he turned back to me.

"Sorry, Lila, it's a brand new Busby Berkeley movie called *Gold Diggers of 1933*. It has all the big stars like Dick Powell, Joan Blondell, Ruby Keeler and even Miss Ginger Rogers."

"I think I've heard of Dick Powell, but not too sure about the others."

"Don't worry. I think the movie will lift your spirits after everything you and your momma have been through."

Peter took the tickets and held my arm as we walked into the theater. Somehow I just knew this would be a night to remember.

Chapter 25

I had been to a picture show only once before, with Momma, many years ago. She always liked Buster Keaton; unfortunately the old Bijou theater that was on the other side of the city had burned down long ago.

Peter told me that this newer theater was like a grand palace, with red carpeting and red velvet seats. We walked in and I saw there were two aisles, down either side. Peter took my hand and led me down the aisle to the right, and chose seats for us in the middle section. Before the movie started, an organist appeared to rise up from the floor on the stage and began playing songs from the movie.

After about thirty minutes, the last song was played, and as the organ disappeared below the stage, the giant red velvet curtain opened, and the picture began to play. I knew many people during these hard times would scrimp and save just for a night out to forget all their troubles. If this movie didn't raise your spirits, nothing would. Each song was wonderful and the dance numbers were a sight to behold.

I noticed that Peter would glance over at me every so often to see how I liked the show, and I think he got his answer when I noticed my jaw dropping every time another dance number came on. Half way through the movie, Peter was fidgeting a little in his seat and then he made his move, and casually put his arm around me. I don't think I had ever felt so secure, even though I had met him only one day ago.

At the end of the movie, the organist reappeared and

played a song called, *We're In The Money*, as people got up from their seats and began to walk out to the street. At least Peter had kept his promise—the rain had stopped, and there was a beautiful full moon.

Once we were outside I realized I had left my purse on my seat inside the theater. "Oh Peter, I must have left my purse on my seat. Why don't you get the car and bring it around, and I'll just run inside and get it. I'll be right back out," I said.

"Okay, Lila. I'll get the car and pick you up right out front," he said.

I ran back inside the theater and found one of the matrons with a flashlight who walked me over to where we had sat. Sure enough, my purse was right where I had left it. I picked it up and headed back outside to meet Peter.

As I walked outside again, I saw a crowd of people standing around, and then I heard a woman scream as the crowd began to converge at the side of the theater. I wasn't sure what all the commotion was about; neither did I see Peter waiting for me in the car in front of the theater.

People were running in every which direction and after I became lost in the crowd that had formed, I asked a man what in tarnation was going on.

"Young Lady, you shouldn't be here," he said.

"Why not, Sir? I just came out of the show and I'm looking for the young man that brought me to see the movie."

"I'm sorry, Miss, but there has been a murder. Seems a young man was found in a car with his throat slashed. Poor guy, looks like he never had a chance."

It was at the very moment that I yelled Peter's name and

began furiously pushing through the crowd. There were four police cars that had just arrived and after finally breaking through the throngs of people, I was in utter shock at what I saw.

There was Peter, with blood all over his shirt and suit, and the police were asking if anyone knew this man. It was if time just stood still. I couldn't speak, and the last thing I remember was everything just going dark.

Chapter 26

The next thing I remembered was a policeman standing over me waving something under my nose. I must have fainted, but whatever I was inhaling woke me up. Then I heard the officer asking me if I knew the victim, but I was sobbing and in such a state of shock at what I had seen that I couldn't speak.

The officer asked me again, "Young lady, do you know who this young man is?"

Still sobbing, I finally told the officer, "His name is Peter Johnston. We had come to see the movie and he was just going to get the car for me."

The officer helped me up off the ground and got me into his patrol car while onlookers kept staring at me. The officer then walked over to a detective who helped him place a white sheet over Peter. Then the detective came to the car I was in and said, "We're going to take a ride to the police station. Don't worry, Miss. You're going to be all right."

On the ride over to the police station, I felt numb and almost paralyzed at the thought that Peter was gone. *How could this be*? I kept asking myself. *This has to be a bad dream*. But sadly, it wasn't a dream. Tonight, my world had come to an end.

I knew the detective was talking to me, but I couldn't utter a word. All I could think about was that wonderful, good-looking young man that I had just met. I kept thinking to myself, *Peter could have been the man of my dreams that finally had come into my life.* And now he was taken away from me.

We soon reached the police station, and as I was escorted in, I noticed a lot of men that had seen better days. There were men with torn clothes, men that were drunk, and some chained to chairs.

I said to the detective, “I don't belong here. Please take me home.”

“I'm sorry, Miss. I can't do that just yet. You’re going to have to answer some questions first,” he said.

We walked upstairs to the detective’s office, with two other detectives coming along. They had me sit in a chair while one of the men took out a large yellow legal pad and began writing. The detective who drove me to the station introduced himself as Detective Ryan, of the Atlanta police department. “Would you like a glass of water?” he asked.

“Yes, I would, please, if you don’t mind.” I answered.

Detective Ryan said that in order to find the killer, they had to ask me some questions.

“How did you know the decedent?”

I looked at detective Ryan and said, “I'm not sure what you mean, Sir. What is a *decedent*?”

“That is a term used to describe someone who has died.” Detective Ryan replied.

“I'm sorry, Sir. I didn't understand that word. Peter came into the Five and Dime that I work at and had lunch yesterday. He came back today and asked if I would like to go to the picture show with him, and I said *yes*.”

“Do you know who he is?” Detective Ryan asked.

"He is Judge Johnston's son, who works at the bank across the street from where I work."

Detective Ryan fell back into his chair with such a strange look on his face. "Are you telling me that young man was Judge Johnston's son? Holy Mary Mother Of God!"

It was then that Detective Ryan asked the other men in the room to look after me as he left to make a call.

I told one of the other detectives I didn't feel so good, and he allowed me to lie down on a leather couch that was in the office. All I could do at that point was lie on my side as I continued to cry, while repeating Peter's name over and over again. When I finally regained my composure, I asked one of the detectives if he could get in touch with my mother.

"Of course, Miss. Don't worry. We can send a car for her. Just give us her name and address."

I provided them with Momma's name and address, and the detective said they would send a car right away to bring her in to the station. I just knew that Momma would be a wreck when the police showed up at the house.

After several minutes, Detective Ryan returned to the office and said that he had contacted the judge's residence, and that the judge was on his way to the station.

My head was reeling, and all I felt was total numbness at the events that had taken place earlier this evening. How could this be? Why would the good Lord allow this to happen? I kept asking myself why this happened, and yet nothing made sense.

Chapter 27

As I waited for Momma to arrive at the police station, I heard voices outside in the hall leading to detective Ryan's office. Then the door opened and a large, well-dressed man in a suit walked in and asked the detective if this was the girl.

"Yes, this is Lila, Judge Johnston."

I knew then that this was Peter's father. He looked at me with a sullen face as he pulled a chair close to the couch I was sitting on. As he sat down, he took my hand and asked, "Are you all right, My Dear?"

All I could do was burst out in tears, and as I leaned forward he held me as I remember my own father did many years ago.

"I'm so sorry, Judge Johnston. This is my fault. I never should have gone to the movies with your son. I know this is entirely my fault."

"There now, Lila. It wasn't your fault. This was the action of someone who is deranged, and whoever it is that did this will be found and prosecuted to the fullest extent of the law."

I kept saying over and over, "This should never have happened. Peter was such a wonderful person."

"Yes, Lila, he was," the judge said. "Do you have any idea who would have done this to my son?"

"I just don't know, Judge Johnston. But in a strange way, maybe this is connected to events that you're already aware of that took place at my Momma's house."

"You mean the broken window, Lila?"

"Yes, Judge," I replied.

"Lila," the judge said, "can you tell me what happened at your house?"

I spent the next two hours telling the judge, as well as the detectives, how I loved to sing with Momma and that there was a man that would stand across the street and listen. "I bumped into him accidentally while going to work one day, and he said his name was *Charles*."

"Was there anything about this man that scared you, Lila?" the judge asked.

"It was strange. When I sang hymns with Momma, he would stand outside and listen. Then one day I asked Momma if she would learn a new song called *Blue Skies*."

"Yes, I'm familiar with that song, Lila," the judge said. Please go on."

"When I went out to buy the sheet music, I bumped into Charles again, and when I told him I had just bought the music to *Blue Skies*, he seemed to change."

"Changed how, Lila?" the judge asked. He looked angry and sad at the same time. "Please continue," the judge suggested.

"Well, I brought the music home and convinced Momma to play it for me. When I began to sing it, I noticed Charles outside, and for some reason he had a stick in his hands that he snapped like a twig. Momma had called me back to the piano, and when I was done I looked out the window again and he was gone. I didn't think anything of it until someone threw the rock through our window that night."

"Please go on, Child," the judge said. Then he looked at Detective Ryan and asked if he was getting all of this.

"The next day I accidentally bumped into Charles and he asked me never to sing that *damn song* again. Then the following day, there was a commotion at the Five and Dime, and my manager, Horace, threw a panhandler out of the store when he couldn't pay for a coffee and a doughnut he had."

"Was that panhandler this *Charles person,* Lila?"

"Yes it was, Judge," I replied.

At that moment, Momma was brought into the office. She obviously was in shock, and sobbing uncontrollably as she asked, in a broken voice, "Lila, are you all right? Are you hurt? Did anyone touch you?"

"No, no, no, Momma, I'm fine. But poor Peter was killed at the movie we went to see."

At that point I jumped up from the couch to hug Momma. The judge had said something to Detective Ryan, and then turned around and said to all of us, "Look, Everyone, it's nearly four in the morning. I think we have had enough for now. Detective Ryan, will you please personally escort these women to their home, and I want a police officer stationed in front and back of their house until this murderer is caught."

"Yes, Your Honor, we'll take care of it immediately."

Chapter 28

Momma and I both thanked Judge Johnston for his help, and before leaving the police station I told him again how sorry I was for his loss.

"Don't worry, Lila. We'll catch and prosecute whoever did this to my son," he said.

Detective Ryan escorted Momma and me down to a waiting police car, with two officers that would stand guard at our home. No one in the car uttered a word all the way home. As Momma held my hand, all I could think of was Peter, and how Momma and I ever could cope with all that had happened that evening. How could I continue with anything? Nothing seemed to matter.

When we reached the house, Detective Ryan asked Momma for the key. He said he would take the two officers with him and search the house to make sure no one was inside. After they were finished, Detective Ryan came out and said it was safe to enter, and told us that the two police officers would be stationed at the front and back of our home.

Momma and I got out of the police car and entered the house. The sun was nearly breaking over the horizon. We both were exhausted from the events of the night and just wanted to get some sleep. Before Detective Ryan left, I asked him if he could stop by the Five and Dime and explain to Mr. Horace Hollis, the store manager, what had happened, and that I wouldn't be in today.

"Yes, Lila, I'll be glad to stop there and explain to him. I'm sure he would not expect you in under the circumstances."

Momma barely said a word. She simply gave me a hug and told me to get some sleep, and said she would be up shortly. After I entered my room I still felt as if time simply had ceased to exist. All I could think of was Peter's smile, and how precious life really is. I began to think that I was the cause of everything that had happened. If it weren't for my singing, none of this would have happened.

Somehow I just knew that Charles was involved in Peter's death. I got undressed and sat in front of my mirror, brushing my hair. As I looked at my emotionless face reflecting back at me, I swore that I would never sing again. That would be my self-imposed punishment, and I believed that was the least I could do in Peter's memory. I wasn't sure how my life would continue, but with Momma's help, I hoped that in time things might return to normal.

About that time Momma knocked on my door and asked if I was all right.

"Yes, Momma, I'm fine. I just want to sleep."

"Okay, Lila," Momma said. "I'll be here if you need anything."

"Thank you, Momma. I'll see you later," I replied.

As I thought of that wonderful young man, I wanted to cry, but there were no tears left to shed. I finally closed my eyes and fell into a deep sleep. I must have slept for five hours, and when I awoke, I heard people talking in the kitchen.

I got dressed and went downstairs and found Momma

with the two police officers sitting around the kitchen table talking. As soon as I walked into the kitchen, they all looked at me and asked how I was feeling.

"I'm just tired. I'm a little thirsty, so I thought I would come down for some lemonade."

The two officers excused themselves and returned to their posts, while I sat down at the kitchen table with Momma.

"Are you really all right, Lila?" Momma asked.

"Momma, I feel so empty inside. How could anyone hurt Peter? He didn't deserve this and I feel as if I'm to blame."

"Lila, you know the good Lord works in mysterious ways. But some day with the passage of time, I hope these memories will fade."

"Momma, I can't explain why, but I just know in my heart I will never sing again. I just know this was entirely my fault."

"Lila, you're just exhausted from everything and all. You'll feel better in a few days' time."

"No, Momma. I'll never sing again. I can't, Momma. I just can't."

I know Momma was worried about me, but nothing seemed to matter any longer. I excused myself and went back to my room. All I wanted to do was sleep.

Chapter 29

Time never stands still, and after a couple of days had passed, I went back to work at the Five and Dime. Momma, bless her heart, continued picking up laundry from Mr. Crawford's bakery, and the two policemen that were stationed at our home were still standing guard just in case Charles decided to show up.

I had never experienced before the kind of emptiness that Peter's death brought on, but I knew in my heart that I would stick to my promise never to sing again. How could I? Had Peter never met me, none of this ever would have happened. Days morphed into weeks, and neither I nor the police ever saw the man again that I had described as Charles. He may well have left the area. He just seemed to be a man with problems from his past, and for the life of me, I never did figure out why the song, *Blue Skies,* seemed to change his demeanor in the blink of an eye.

It had been a month now since Peter's murder, and life was beginning to return to normal. The two police officers that stood guard at our home had left after three weeks. Detective Ryan stoppd by occasionally to look in on Momma and me. But any leads the police had just seemed to take them to more dead ends. Detective Ryan said there probably wasn't anything to be concerned about, as this man, Charles, probably had boarded one of the many trains that passed through and just left town the same way he had arrived.

We were well into the month of September, the time of year that the rainy season brought the potential for a hurricane to rush up the coast. Atlanta saw its fair share of storms during this time, but regardless, come rain or shine, there was still laundry to get done, and I was still working for Horace at the Five and Dime.

One day Horace asked me if I could work an evening shift, as the woman who worked the register after I left for the day was scheduled for a day off, as she had to attend to her mother, who was ill.

I told Horace, "Sure. I'll be happy to. When would you need me?" I asked.

"Lila, it will be this Friday evening, if that's okay with you," he said.

"Sure, Horace," I said. "I just need to tell Momma that I I'll have to work late that evening."

I thought for a moment, and realized that working Friday evening would mean I would have to walk to work in the dark. But since Charles seemed to have disappeared, there was really nothing to fear, so I just never gave it much thought, and planned to head to the store after Momma and I finished dinner that evening.

Chapter 30

On Friday there was a terrible rainstorm that had come up from the south. I finished dinner with Momma and helped clean up the dishes before heading back to my room to get changed and ready for work. I couldn't quite place why I felt as I did, but for some reason, I just had this uneasiness about me. It probably was just my overactive imagination, coupled with the howling wind and rain outside.

After getting dressed I tied my hair into a ponytail and as I sat in front of my mirror, I listened to the sound the wind made as it blew through cracks around my window frame. It was a strange, high-pitched sound that would get louder and softer depending on how hard the wind was blowing. Then I began to think about the events that had taken place more than a month ago. But I took some solace in knowing that Charles was long gone from the area, and that the police would eventually catch up with him and bring him to justice.

As I left my room I heard Momma practicing on the piano in the parlor. She stopped as I walked in, and asked if I would be all right walking down to the store at night.

"I'll be fine, Momma. I really think that man, Charles, is long gone," I told her. "At least no one has seen him for quite a while. I'd better get going, and I'll check with you when I get back home."

I gave momma a kiss and headed out into the storm with an old umbrella we had.

I walked as fast as I could, but at times the wind was so strong it actually would stop me in my tracks for a moment. As I came around the corner, I saw the light blazing in the store. Friday night was the only night the store was open late. Horace knew it was payday for many of the customers that came in, and he always figured it was the best day to have a sale, as people would have more money to spend.

Olivia was working the counter and it was pretty busy, considering how the skies had opened up. The rain and the wind just never let up, and many people stopped in just to get a cup of coffee. I noticed that many of them, after paying their bill, would then walk around the store to check out the various items that were on sale. I had to hand it to Horace. As a store manager he had people pretty well figured out, and the weather seemed to be driving people right into the place just to get out of the rain.

I had to work only four hours, and people were leaving the store as Horace began to shut off some of the lights in the rear of the store, which I think was his way of letting people know that the store was getting ready to close. People began to run up to the register in the front of the store to pay for their purchases, and then head out into the night on their way back to their homes. It wasn't long before I was saying goodnight to Horace and Olivia, as I also would soon be on my way back home.

I brought my register drawer back to the manager's office to be locked in the safe for the night, and then grabbed my poor excuse of an umbrella and was getting ready to head out the front door, when Horace yelled for me to wait a minute. I thought to myself, *I must have done something wrong*, but to my surprise, as Horace walked toward me, he held out a brand new umbrella to give to me.

"Lila," Horace said, "I don't know how you managed to keep yourself dry with that broken-down umbrella you came in with. So here's a brand new one, free of charge, on the house."

"Oh thank you, Horace. I didn't really think my old umbrella would make it, but had no idea anyone had noticed. You're so thoughtful. How can I ever thank you enough?" I asked.

"Don't worry about it," Horace replied, with a big smile. "Just get yourself home safe, Lila, and this new umbrella should keep you nice and dry."

I thanked Horace again and went on my way through the wind and rain back to the house. The storm must have brought down some of the electric poles, as the lights on two of the streets I had to walk through were dark. I guess I would just have to walk a little faster. As I came around the corner onto one of the darkened streets, I suddenly had that very strange and sickening feeling again that someone was watching me. I refused to let my imagination run away with me, and just walked even faster.

The rain was pelting me so hard along with the heavy gusts of wind that I decided to duck into an alley just to catch my breath and get a break from the wind. I stood under a window that had a cloth awning over it, which also gave me shelter from the rain.

As I peered out into the street again, there wasn't another soul to be seen—and then it happened! I felt a man's hand take hold of my arm, and before I could let out a scream, he had placed his other hand over my mouth. At that moment I could hardly breathe and really panicked.

Chapter 31

"Laura, listen to my voice. I'm going to count backwards from five to one, and when I reach one, you're going to be able to open your eyes and feel completely relaxed. Five, four, three, two, one. Now open your eyes, Laura."

As I opened my eyes I felt as if someone had their hands around my neck, and I knew from my breathing that I must have been close to hyperventilating.

My psychiatrist, Dr. David Morrissey, was holding my hand, asking if I could recall what had happened during my first past-life regression session with him. It took me a moment to compose my thoughts, and slowly memories began to flood back into my consciousness. It was as if I had been reliving an event that had taken place many years ago. It just seemed so real.

"Laura, here's a glass of water. Why don't you sit up and take a sip," he said.

"My heart is still pounding, Dr. Morrissey, although I'm not sure what it was I experienced."

"That's not uncommon, Laura, especially after a regression in which it seems that bodily harm may have taken place. When you came to me, Laura, do you recall the original reason you had sought my help?" he asked.

"Yes, Dr. Morrissey. It seemed so silly at the time, yet it always bothered me as to why I had seemed to have developed a phobia to singing."

"Well, Laura, there have been many cases where an individual has experienced a traumatic event in a past life that on some occasions will carry over into a patient's current life. In your case, it seems that there was some event that took place in a past life, and for some reason it is affecting you in your current life. I believe after a few more sessions we'll be able to find out what that event was, and once you understand how and why you have this fear of singing, we should finally be able to put this matter to rest."

"Thank you, Dr. Morrissey. I believe a lot of people might think something like this is crazy. I mean, to think that a soul from one person having lived many years ago could come to evolve again in another life. That's just a lot to take in," I said.

"Not really, Laura. There have been many documented cases where a soul's physical life ends and then transfers from one life to the next in a different physical form while trying to correct or change in some way what had happened in a previous life. Considering the session we've already had, in a past life, you were this girl named *Lila*, who apparently went through a difficult time during the Great Depression. What we don't know yet is what happened to her. Perhaps we can get to the bottom of it in a few more sessions."

"Thank you, Dr. Morrissey. I guess it makes sense, and yet at the same time it doesn't. But I'm willing to see where this goes. See you next Thursday?"

"Yes, Laura. Let's make it at ten Thursday morning," the doctor replied.

After what seemed like a terrifying session with the doctor, I had to catch up with my high school girlfriend,

Beth, for lunch. We had been best friends for years, and this was going to be one fantastic story to tell her. Knowing Beth, she probably would think I was totally losing it, but she was a lot of fun to be around, and since we both worked for the same law firm, we always had the chance to talk.

Chapter 32

I caught up with Beth at one of our favorite restaurants in the Big Apple, *Le Bernadin*, on West 51st Street. Sure enough, there she was at our table sipping on a martini. As I walked over to her, she smiled and asked how things went with the doctor.

"It was really very strange, Beth," I said. "By the way how many of those martinis have you had?"

"Oh, I've lost count, Laura. Why not just pull up a chair and join me so you can fill me in on all the gory details."

When our waiter came over to take my order, I said to him, "I'll have what she's having, and make it extra dry, please."

Then I turned back to Beth when she asked, "So, are you going to spill the beans?"

"I have to tell you, Beth, the strangest thing happened at our session today. After the doctor hypnotized me, I was regressed back to a previous life. I can't really remember everything, but it was during the time of the Great Depression, and my name was *Lila.* Something traumatic happened to me then, but at this point I'm not sure what it was."

"Laura, that sounds fascinating. Does the doctor really think that this has something to do with your fear of singing?" Beth asked.

"I guess in some strange way it could. Dr. Morrissey

believes we can get to the bottom of it with just a few more sessions. So I'm game to find out why I always have had such a terrible fear of singing."

"Maybe I should try this doctor out and get regressed myself. I've always had a fear of heights. Maybe in a past life I was a high-wire act and fell to my death or something," Beth said.

"Oh, stop being silly," I said, with a smile. "Just how many of those martinis did you say you've had?"

Beth and I, now in our forties, were both off from work on the same day—luckily for her, as she would never be able to function after the martinis she was putting away. But good old Beth was always a lot of fun, and you couldn't have asked for a better friend in life. We spent the next hour going over some of the information that had come out of my past life regression with Dr. Morrissey, and then we went our separate ways to take care of chores we each had to do.

"Beth, I'll give you a call later this evening. Okay, Girl?"

"Great," Beth said. "Talk to you later."

As I headed back to my apartment, I kept thinking about what had happened at the doctor's office earlier. I tried making sense of what little I knew, but I certainly was very interested in moving forward with this, as I really had to get to the bottom of this crazy fear of singing I had had all of my life.

Once I arrived back home, I kicked off my *Manolo Blahnik* heels that were killing me, and collapsed on the couch. Something inside of me just seemed to tell me that I was going to find the answers I was looking for, yet there was still another part of me that said this was just totally crazy—unless I could find some way to verify the story that seemed to be developing through these sessions. What I needed were facts, like dates, names and places. If there was really anything to this past life regression stuff, then surely I could corroborate what Dr. Morrissey was getting me to talk about.

Chapter 33

It was busy as usual at the law firm. Beth and I, as legal secretaries, always had case files to catch up on, but I couldn't get my mind off of what had transpired with Dr. Morrissey and my past-life regression. Could there really be something to this? Maybe it was the fact that I always had worked around lawyers who dug for the truth that was inspiring me to move forward with these regressions. Tomorrow would be my second session and I was becoming really fascinated, wanting to know more about what this person, Lila, had gone through.

The next day, as I was approaching the doctor's office, my mind was racing with anticipation as to how and where this story about Lila was going. I took a deep breath as I entered the elevator to make my way to his office. I was right on time, as Dr. Morrissey's last patient was just leaving.

"Good morning, Laura," he said. "Are we ready for our next session?"

"Yes, Dr. Morrissey. I've been thinking about this for the last week, and hopefully I'm getting closer to understanding this phobia I seem to have."

"Laura, make yourself comfortable on the couch and we can begin."

The doctor's couch was really quite comfortable, and given that I had been hypnotized previously, it seemed easier this time to slip into a state of total relaxation. The last thing I remember before going under was my eyes growing heavy, and then a feeling of total peace.

"Laura," the doctor said, "I would like you to go back in time. Go back to the time and place where you were first aware of the girl named Lila."

As I listened to the doctor guide me through the regression, I could almost feel the heat of the Atlanta sun on my skin. "Where are you now, Laura?" the doctor asked.

As I began to speak, it was a strange feeling being my physical self, and yet I heard myself speaking with a distinctive southern drawl.

"I'm in the deep south. I'm in Atlanta, Georgia. It is time to leave work at the Five and Dime and I have stopped for a moment to look at a newspaper that a customer left behind. It's September of 1933, and I'm reading about the murder of a young man, Peter Johnston. "Oh my God. Peter, I'm so sorry. I'm so sorry that any of this happened," I heard myself saying.

I could hear Dr. Morrissey's voice as he guided me. "It's all right, Laura, you're totally safe. How were you connected to this person, Peter Johnston?" he asked.

"I had met this nice young man a few days before, when he came into the store for lunch and asked me out to a picture show."

"Did you go to the show with Peter, Lila?" the doctor asked.

"Yes, he picked me up in his new car that he got as a graduation present from his father."

"Lila, can you tell me what happened after the show was over?" Dr. Morrissey asked.

"Why yes. After the picture was over, we walked outside, and then I noticed that I had left my purse on the seat back in the theater. I told Peter to bring the car around while I went back in to fetch my purse."

"After you retrieved your purse, did you go back out to the street to meet Peter?" the doctor asked.

"Yes, I did, but Peter wasn't there. All I saw was a large crowd standing around and then I heard a woman scream. I stopped a man and asked what all the commotion was about and he said that a young man's throat had been slashed."

"Go on, Lila," the doctor said.

"I made my way through the crowd, and then I saw Peter. Oh my God, how can this be happening? It's Peter! There's blood all over his clothes. No! No! This can't be happening."

"Try to relax, Lila. Can you tell me what happened next?" the doctor asked.

"I'm not rightly sure. The next thing I remember was someone helping me up off the street. I think I had passed out from the shock of seeing that poor young man dead and all."

"Lila, you mentioned the young man's name. You said it was Peter Johnston. Is that correct?"

"Yes, that's right. His father was a judge in the city of Atlanta, and the judge came to see me at the police station."

"Lila, let's leave the police station and move forward in time about a month. You said you were working during a bad storm and then you were heading home. Is that correct?" the doctor asked.

"Yes. It was a terrible storm, and the manager of the store gave me a brand new umbrella to take with me."

"Lila, do you remember what happened to you as you walked back home?" the doctor asked.

"I was half way home, and just wanted to stop for a minute. I slipped into an alley and stood under a window awning. It was then that I felt a very uneasy presence, and before I knew what was happening, a man grabbed me by my arm and clamped his hand over my mouth. I couldn't scream, and it was difficult to breath. All I could think of at the moment was that I knew this man and he was hurting me."

"Lila, you're completely safe with me. Please continue," the doctor said.

"I'm so afraid. I know who this man is. It's the same man that stood outside my momma's window. Every time I would sing while Momma played the piano, the man would just stand across the street and listen."

"Then what happened, Lila. as the man listened to you sing?" the doctor asked.

"One day, I asked Momma if she would learn a new song for me called *Blue Skies*. The first time I sang the song, I noticed the same man standing outside our window across the street and then a strange thing happened."

"What was that, Lila?" the doctor asked.

"He had a stick in his hand and he broke it in half. After I had finished the song, I looked out the window, but the man was gone. You're hurting me, please stop!"

"Who's hurting you, Lila?" the doctor asked.

"It's him! It's Charles! The same man that stood in the street. He's choking me. I'm trying to fight him off, but, but he's too strong, I can't."

"Laura, I want you to relax now. Take a deep breath and

listen to my voice. I'm going to count from five to one and when I reach one, you'll be able to open your eyes and you'll feel totally relaxed and refreshed as if you had just come back from a great vacation. Five, four, three, two, one. Now open your eyes, Laura."

Chapter 34

After the regression was over, I sat up on the couch and Dr. Morrissey handed me a glass of water. "How are you feeling, Laura, the doctor asked?"

"Honestly, I feel like I've just had the crap kicked out of me. What took place, Dr. Morrissey? Are we getting any answers yet?" I asked.

"Well, Laura, this story is coming into great focus now. In one of your past lives, your name was *Lila.* and apparently you loved to sing while your mother played the piano. This life story of Lila seems to take place in 1933 in Atlanta, Georgia, during the Great Depression."

"This is simply amazing, Dr. Morrissey. Then I guess I can at least make the connection that in a past life I did love to sing. Correct?" I asked.

"It seems that way, Laura. But there was a significant emotional trauma that took place. Do you recall what it was?"

"Why yes, I believe I do. A young man I went out with by the name of Peter was murdered, I think. And then there was something about walking home, and I believe I was attacked by someone."

"Yes, Laura. You said the man that attacked you was named *Charles*. Does that mean anything to you?"

"At this point, not really, Dr. Morrissey, but I am

certainly willing to follow through with this and find out what happened. Let's give this another shot next week. Okay, Dr. Morrissey?"

"Yes, Laura. Let's make it the same time next week," he said.

I felt somewhat composed after finishing our session, and as I left the doctor's office, I thought I really was getting closer to the answers I had been looking for. I knew Beth was never going believe this story, but there had to be something to this past-life regression business. I had never been in the city of Atlanta in my life, so how could I possibly know about events that took place back in 1933?

At the least, I now had names, places, and dates, and as long as it was my day off, I had an idea of what I wanted to do. I decided to head to the main branch of the New York Public Library. Maybe I could find some answers to questions I had in reading stories from old newspapers that were available on microfilm in the library's vast archive. At least it was worth at shot.

As I arrived at the library, I made my way to the newspaper archives and began a search of some of the local newspapers that were in circulation at the time. I found a newspaper called the *Courier-Times*. Then I looked at dates from the summer of 1933. The first thing I wanted to check was the obituaries during the month of August. As I was scrolling through names, my jaw dropped when I saw the name, *Peter Johnston*, the same name that had come up in my past-life regression!

How could this be? Was it actually possible to be regressed back to a time in a past life where one could unravel issues that affected people in their current life? There must have been something to all of this, and I was hell-bent to get to the bottom of this story and how it may well have been affecting me some eighty-two years later.

With each regression session, I felt I was getting closer to the answers I was looking for. But I also noticed that after each session, I was feeling increasingly emotionally drained, and just wasn't sure I could see this project along to its conclusion. Yet, some little voice inside me kept prompting me to move forward. I just had to resolve this matter, one way or the other.

Chapter 35

When I returned home I began going through photo copies of the pages from the Atlanta newspaper I had made at the library, where I had found the obituary of Peter Johnston. Damn! I didn't go far enough in my search. All I could find were accounts of what had happened that evening in 1933. I knew I had to go back to the library and keep digging, as I had to know what the final outcome was for Lila. Did she escape her captor, or could Lila have met the same fate that her friend, Peter, did. I just had to know the answer before getting into my next session with Dr. Morrissey.

It was getting late, and I was just totally exhausted from the day's events. I really wanted to get back to the library, but had to be at work early the following day. So I decided just to let it go for now and turn in for the night. As I was drifting off to sleep, the strangest feeling came over me. It was almost as if someone was standing at the foot of my bed.

I arose from my bed and looked around. I thought for a moment I was losing it, when suddenly I heard music playing in the living room. Then I remembered I had turned the stereo on while I was reading through some of the copies I made at the library, and I must have forgotten to turn it off prior to going to bed.

Sure enough, as I made my way back to the living room, the stereo was playing. Just as I reached to turn the stereo off, I realized the song playing sounded vaguely familiar—like a song that my grandmother used to listen to. I think it was on one of those old 78 records that people used to play on phonographs.

I stood there listening until the end, assuming the announcer would mention the song's name when it was over. When the announcer spoke again, and revealed the name of the song, it sent chills running down my spine. The song was *Blue Skies*, the same song that the young girl, Lila, was singing when that man, Charles, snapped that stick in half and then took off.

There was no way I was going to get to sleep after that. I turned the stereo off and poured myself a stiff drink and began writing down notes. I had to discuss this with Dr. Morrissey the next time we met. I looked over at the clock on my desk and suddenly realized it was already after two in the morning, and I had to be at work at eight. At least the vodka was working its magic, and I began to feel drowsy enough to call it a night.

I tried to gather my thoughts and then just sat back in my chair, staring aimlessly into space. What in the world would be the odds of hearing the very song on my stereo that Lila had sung so many decades ago? For some strange reason the word synchronicity just popped into my head. This was beyond coincidence, I thought. Either that or I was just letting my imagination run away with me.

I pushed my notes to the side of my desk and decided to crawl back into bed. I just needed to shut down my rather analytical brain for the night, as nothing really was making sense to me. I closed my eyes and before I knew it, the damned clock radio was going off at six-thirty. Where did the night go, I wondered. I was exhausted, but hoped at least a quick shower would bring me back to the land of the living. I just couldn't get the events of the night before out of my mind, and I knew it was going to be a long day at the office.

Chapter 36

I reached the office in the nick of time. I'm convinced the New York traffic must truly exist to drive people mad. As I rushed to catch an elevator, there was Beth, standing against the back wall, looking at me through her sunglasses.

"What's up, Girl?" she asked.

"Beth," I whispered, "you're never going to believe what happened to me last night."

"Oh, tell me, tell me. Was he a great looking guy?" she asked.

"No, Silly. I think it was better than a one-night stand."

"Really, My Dear? What drugs were you taking?" she asked, with a brief laugh.

When we finally made it to our floor I told Beth I would catch up with her at lunch. As I took my seat at my desk, I saw I had a ton of paper work to get through and got started on it the moment I sat down. I was either on caffeine overload, or just caught my second wind, but I simply felt very energized.

It's funny how some days seem to move faster than others. Before I knew it, it was already noon. Beth came over to my section of the office complex and asked if I was still planning on filling her in.

Wow! It's time for lunch already? I thought.

Beth continued, "Look, we have an hour to kill, so let's grab something to eat and you can tell me all about your wonderful night."

"Wonderful?" I replied. I don't know about *wonderful*, but it definitely fits into the category of the *strange*, for sure," I said.

We headed down to the ground floor and then walked to a little place that made some of the best wraps in the city. After we got our order, we found a table for two in the rear. "You're never going to believe this," I said to Beth.

"Well, Laura, are you just going to flap your gums, or are you going to tell me what happened?" Beth prompted.

I looked at Beth and asked her if she believed in the afterlife.

"You mean like dead people coming back to life?" she asked.

"Something like that," I said. "I had my second regression session with Dr. Morrissey yesterday, and there seems to be a story evolving around a guy, Peter Johnston, that was murdered back in 1933 in Atlanta, Georgia."

"How could you possibly know about something that happened that far back?" Beth queried.

"Well, it seems that during this past-life regression, I somehow thought I was a girl named *Lila*, who loved to sing. So far, that's the only connection I've made other than some information I found at the library."

"What kind of information, Laura?" Beth asked.

"Well, Beth, I was searching old newspapers and found the obituary for Peter Johnston, who apparently had his throat slashed, and this girl, Lila, seemed to be involved in all this in some way."

"Now you're freaking me out, Laura," Beth said. "Are you sure you want to continue digging into this?"

"Beth, I have to. I always have had this crazy fear of singing, and somehow there seems to be a soul connection between me and this girl, Lila. And this even gets stranger, Beth," I said.

"How so, Girlfriend?" Beth asked.

"I know this is going to sound bizarre, but during my last regression, I had told the doctor, as Lila, that there was a song my mother played called *Blue Skies*. Then after I came home from the library, I had begun writing some notes for my next session, and then just wanted to get to sleep. I got into bed and had this strange feeling that someone was standing at the foot of my bed. There wasn't anyone but me in the apartment, and then I heard music playing from the living room.

I thought I probably had forgotten to turn off the stereo, so I got up and went into the living room to shut it off. That's when I heard this song playing that sounded familiar to me. No singing, just the melody. Something my grandmother used to play. After it was over, the announcer came on and said the name of the song was *Blue Skies*. Beth, I thought I was going to soil my drawers on the spot."

For a moment, Beth just stared at me with her mouth open. "Are you freaking kidding me?" Beth said.

"No, I'm not kidding you," I replied. "At that moment the word *synchronicity* popped into my head. So I just wrote a bunch of notes to bring with me to the doctor on my next visit to see if we can make any sense out of what is happening."

"Laura, I've heard some stories in my life, and if I didn't know you for as long as I have, I would think you were crazy. Shit like this just doesn't happen every day," Beth said.

"I know, Beth," I replied. "I just want to get to the bottom of this, and maybe in the end, actually solve the original problem I sought out Dr. Morrissey to help me with.

"Oh crap. Look at the time," I said to Beth. "We'd better get back to the office."

"Laura, you're working on how many hours of sleep?" Beth asked.

"I think about four, and that reminds me. I want to buy one of those energy drinks loaded with caffeine, otherwise I'll never make it through the rest of the day."

Chapter 37

We got back to the office and it looked as though I had plowed through the day's work in record time. I just had to get back to the library and do a little more digging, but I was afraid I wouldn't have enough time before it closed if I waited until I got off from work. I needed a way to get out of the office for the afternoon. I pulled the energy drink out of my purse and drank it. Since there wasn't anything left on my desk to complete, I decided to talk to my supervisor and just tell her I wasn't feeling well after lunch. Luckily for me, since I was all caught up, she didn't have any problem in letting me go for the rest of the day.

I stopped off to talk to Beth and told her I was leaving for the rest of the day, having given the head secretary a story about not feeling well.

"I know where you're going," Beth volunteered.

"Just keep your big mouth shut, Beth," I said, with a slightly devious grin. "I have to find out more, and I'm heading to the library. I'll give you a call later this evening."

I left the building as fast as I could and made my way back to the library. I pulled up the paper I had been reading the day before and found the obituary again. From there, I kept searching for any information on the death of Peter Johnston, and finally I found what I was looking for. I made several more copies of the newspaper pages, and couldn't wait to get back home so I could dive into this story.

Was any of this making sense? Where was all of this leading? So many loose strings to tie together. With the past-life regressions, the music that was playing the night before, and what I had found at the library, I just felt that it all had to be tied together. One way or the other, I was going to get to the bottom of what I had discovered, and soon I would have my answer.

It was nearly four p.m. by the time I had returned to my apartment, and after kicking off my shoes, I noticed the light on the answering machine was flashing. Sure enough, it was Beth. She just wanted to know what else I had dug up in my evolving mystery. I could easily put Beth off a few hours, as I really wanted to read up on the articles I had copied from the library.

With papers in hand, I sat at my desk and started at the beginning. This poor guy, Peter Johnston, had been brutally murdered when someone slashed his throat, and Lila Hartley was with him that same evening. I continued sifting through the copies as I was looking for what happened. Did the authorities ever catch the murderer? What happened to Lila afterwards? It was then that I came across a follow-up to this unfolding story.

According to the follow-up story, neither the murder weapon nor the murderer was ever found. Even stranger, in late September of 1933, another article appeared in the paper stating that several days after Peter's death, Miss Hartley went missing. As I continued reading, I learned that there was a fire that destroyed an old abandoned house on the outskirts of the city, where two bodies were found. Apparently the fire broke out after the house was struck by lightning. One of the bodies was a young man in his thirties by the name of Charles Sycamore. Police identified the man after finding a wallet containing newspaper clippings about the stockmarket crash of 1929 in which he, as a stockbroker, had lost everything, including his wife, in an eventual divorce. Then the poor guy apparently lost his life when a beam in the house that had caught fire collapsed on him, crushing him to death.

As I continued reading, police stated that there was a second body found in the debris of the house. The body seemed to be burned beyond any recognition. Investigators did say, however, that it was a young female in her twenties that was found tied to a chair with a gag in her mouth. Police eventually assumed it was Miss Hartley, because her mother recognized a small, charred swatch of the girl's favorite dress that was white with faded yellow roses.

I thought for a moment how difficult it must have been back in the day to make a positive identification of a body without the modern day advances in DNA technology. But yet, even with the meager amount of clues, the Atlanta police were able to make the connection.

As I continued reading, I came across Lila Hartley's obituary. What was left of the body was buried in a small rural cemetery where the family had a modest plot. The only other mention of what had happened was a story about Lila's mother. It seems that Judge Johnston, Peter Johnston's father, had paid for all the funeral arrangements for Lila.

At this point I needed a stiff drink. All the pieces seemed to be falling in place. Yet, it really didn't bring any resolution for me as to why I had this terrible phobia of singing. I didn't believe that going back to the library again would bring me any closer to finding the answers I was looking for, so that would be a dead end. No, if I were going to get to the bottom of this fear I had, it probably would come from additional regression sessions with Dr. Morrissey. I would be meeting again with him in just a couple more days. Perhaps the next session would shed greater light on what had happened so many years ago. But I was still uncertain as to how whatever transpired then could possibly affect me in the here and now.

Chapter 38

When I got out of bed the next morning, I had a pounding headache, so I popped a couple of Advil's and jumped into the shower. The water felt so good and yet it couldn't wash away the thought of that poor girl being burned alive. I could only imagine the pain her mother must have felt after all the family had already gone through. It just didn't seem fair that Lila's life would end as it did.

After drying off, I got dressed and made my way to the office. I knew Beth would probably be waiting there to drill me, but I had a feeling she probably had found what she had been looking for in male company, and probably had been having a grand old time since she never called back.

As I got off the elevator I began to walk out and then caught sight of Beth walking out of another elevator. "Hey Girl," I said. "Busy night?"

Beth turned and smiled. "You know, Laura, we should always stay the age we are," Beth said.

"What brought that on?" I asked.

With a twinkle in her eye she replied, "You have to get them when they're young. They just love trying out a new position from the *Kama Sutra*," she said with a laugh.

"You bad girl, I said."

"So, are you going to fill me in on what you found on your excursion to the library?" Beth asked.

"We can talk over lunch, Beth, but this story is getting more bizarre by the day and I have to see the doctor again tomorrow. So I'm hoping I'll get back into the past-life regression and be able to tie all these loose ends together."

As we walked into the office I couldn't believe the stack of papers that were waiting for me.

"Have fun with that, Laura. I'll catch you later for lunch," Beth said, as she walked over to her own desk. Being a legal secretary had its ups and down's, but it paid very well and after being with the firm for nearly ten years, I wasn't going anywhere. I guess we all get into a rut at times. We bust our asses for the firm and then get to become full-blown hedonists for four weeks out of the year that we get for a vacation. At least I knew my position was secure as far as the long haul was concerned.

When noon arrived, I saw Beth making her way over to me so we could head out for lunch. We made a beeline over to a little hole in the wall that made the best pizza in the city. There were only a couple of small tables in the place and fortunately we were able to get one of them.

"So Laura, tell me, tell me, what per chance did you find out at the library," Beth asked.

"Beth, I'm not even sure where to start," I replied. "I went back into the archives of the Atlanta newspaper and found Peter Johnston's obituary, and then followed the story from there. It seems a brief time after the murder of this guy, Peter, the young girl, Lila, suddenly disappeared. Apparently, there was a fire in an abandoned house that was caused by a lightning strike and a man by the name of Charles Sycamore was found crushed to death by a ceiling beam that had fallen during the fire."

"But what happened to this girl, Lila? Beth asked.

"So, this is where the story gets a little more gruesome," I replied. It seems a second body of a young woman was also found. She was bound and gagged. The body was pretty badly burned, but a shred of the girls dress was identified by the girl's mother. What a terrible way to go!"

"I'll say," Beth said. "Was there anything else?"

"Not really, Beth, but there has to be some connection to what happened back then as well as that song that keeps popping up in my life."

"Oh, you mean that song, *Blue Skies*?" Beth asked.

"Yes, that one," I replied."

"Honestly, this is going to drive me crazier than I am, but I'm hoping that Dr. Morrissey will be able to help me fill in the blanks and finally resolve this issue I have about this crazy fear of singing."

"Is there a medical term for that, Laura?" Beth asked.

"It's called *decantophobia*, Beth," I said. "Not sure why the medical profession has to use these Latin word roots. It's almost as bad as the jargon we use in our own profession," I said.

"We'd better get back before we're missed. Finish up and let's hit the road, Girl."

Chapter 39

After we had returned to work, I found several ASAP case files that had to be completed, but at least it made the clock on the wall move a whole lot faster. Four o'clock came soon enough, and I couldn't wait to get out of the place, as I was anxious to head back to my apartment and re-read some of the notes I had written down the evening before. I knew there had to be some connection to the events that took place decades ago, and given my nature to turn into a junkyard dog, I was going find out what it was. I told Beth I was going to spend the night in, as I wanted to prepare what information I was able to gather and have it organized when I saw Dr. Morrissey again. I wondered if he was going think I was a nut case, but it didn't matter. I just knew that there had to be a connection with both past and present-day events.

On my way home, I stopped off at a local deli. I didn't really feel like cooking—I was just too engrossed at the thought of finally getting some answers. I picked up a pre-made frozen entree of stuffed shells along with a head of Boston lettuce for a salad, and then made my way to my apartment.

Once I was home, I threw the shells into the microwave, prepared a light salad, and brought everything over to my desk where I had placed all of my notes from the library. As I sat reading, I found myself so involved in Lila's story that half my meal never even made it into my mouth. As I read, I would bring my fork to my face, but ended up missing my mouth and hitting my chin with the food. Okay, you have to do one thing at a time, or you're going to starve to death. I placed the papers down and just concentrated on eating. Once that was out of the way, I got back into the newspaper articles.

Considering the very graphic description of the murder scene, I could almost smell the charred wood in that abandoned house. I closed my eyes and could envision that poor girl burning to death along with her screams for help. I could only imagine how Lila's mother had felt when she learned that her child had been murdered by some deranged lunatic, just as the judge must have felt when he learned of Peter's stabbing. It was all so real to me, and yet I still couldn't fit the pieces of this puzzle together to make any sense of how these events were tied to the phobia I had about singing.

I put the articles down on my desk and just sat there staring out of the window. I just seemed overtaken at the moment with the thought that everyone in life had a story to tell. This story about Lila's short life and that of her new friend, Peter, probably had been replayed a thousand times in different ways in so many households. It's strange, though, that watching the daily news on television and witnessing modern day traumas just didn't seem to resonate with me. I always found myself being drawn back to a different place and time, back to a time in American history when the country was at its lowest. The masses for the most part had lost everything during the Great Depression, and to hear these specific stories like Lila's put an all-too-human face to these events.

I cleaned up after dinner and decided to make it an early night again. I had to be at Dr. Morrissey's office at ten the following morning. I couldn't wait for tomorrow to come, as I felt it might bring some of the answers I was seeking.

Chapter 40

At six-thirty my alarm went off as usual. I was determined that today was going to provide at least some of the answers to questions I had been looking for. As I sat on the edge of my bed, I was hard pressed to forget the image of Lila perishing in that fire, all alone. Her mother must have been beside herself with grief, as any mother would at the loss of a child. As I gathered my thoughts, I began to get ready for my appointment with Dr. Morrissey. After showering, I got dressed, made a cup of coffee and just about inhaled one of New York's famous bagels with cream cheese. As I sat watching one of the morning news shows, I just couldn't get the thought of Lila out of my head. How could I even recount what had happened eighty-plus years ago unless there were some connection that souls make from one life to the next? These were just some of the questions I had for the good doctor.

It was now nearly nine-thirty, so I decided to get myself going, as this was one appointment I didn't want to be late for. I lived up on East Fifty-Second Street and First Avenue, and had to catch a bus down to East Forty-First Street. No need to rush, as the buses ran pretty much on schedule, and there was plenty of time to get to where I had to be. I arrived at my stop with ten minutes to spare, and made my way across the street to the doctors' office building. With each step I took, I just felt that I was getting closer and closer to finding answers to my questions. I knew Dr. Morrissey was one of the best in his field when it came to past-life regressions. Now the articles I had in hand would lend further credence to the belief that we can connect through hypnosis to those lives we have lived prior to the present one we are living. I was pumped and ready to get into another session.

As I entered the doctor's office, the secretary told me the doctor would be with me shortly, but before she had uttered her last word, the doctor entered the waiting room and welcomed me.

"So Laura, how has your week been going?" he asked.

All I could say was, "I'm a believer."

The doctor looked at me quizzically and asked, "What have you been up to, Laura?"

I replied, "You're never going to believe this, but on a hunch, after our last session, I went to the main branch of the public library. I went to the archives room and began looking up old newspaper stories from Atlanta in the summer of 1933. Sure enough, I found the obituary for Peter Johnston, and a whole lot more."

"I guess this makes a believer out of you after all, Laura. I know many have a hard time trying to understand this form of psychiatry, but it is very real and you obviously have validated what has been coming out of our sessions. Would you like to go under now? Perhaps we can flesh out a bit more information and then come to some understanding as to why you have this fear of singing," he said.

"Sure, Dr. Morrissey. Let's do this."

I got myself comfortable on his couch and while listening to his very mellow voice give me instructions, I felt myself slipping away into an incredibly deep and restful sleep.

"Laura," the doctor said, "I want you to go back in time. The year is 1933, and you're living in Atlanta. You're making your way home during a rainstorm when you suddenly are attacked by someone that has his hands around your neck. Can you tell me what happened next, Laura?"

"My name isn't Laura, its *Lila*. I can't breathe. He's holding his hands on my throat."

"Who is, Lila? Who is this man that's hurting you?" the doctor asked.

"I don't know who it is, because I can't see him, and I feel as if I'm going to pass out."

"Lila, can you tell me what happens next?" the doctor asked.

"I'm being carried somewhere. The person who is doing this placed me in a large burlap sack, the kind that potatoes would be delivered in. I'm awake now and screaming for help. Please, please don't hurt me. I feel the sack drop to the floor and now he is hitting me."

"Who is hitting you, Lila? Is it this person who grabbed you off the street?"

"Yes. I felt a sharp blow to my head, now I am waking up. I'm tied to a chair with some type of rag stuffed into my mouth."

"Lila," the doctor asked, "can you see who this man is?"

"Yes, I can. It is the same man that stood outside my window as I would sing with Momma. His name is *Charles*. There's a terrible storm outside and the thunder and lightning is deafening. I'm so scared and so alone."

"Lila, can you tell me what the man is doing now?" the doctor asked.

"He's sitting at an old wooden table and he has a knife. I think he's going to hurt me. I can't speak because he has something in my mouth."

"Then what happens, Lila?" the doctor asked.

He looked at me and then in a fit of rage, drove the knife into the table. He's getting up. He said he would be right back to take care of me because I didn't listen to him. I think he was upset that I kept singing that beautiful song, *Blue Skies*."

"What happens next, Lila?"

"There is a terrible explosion and a brilliant flash of light. Lightning hit the house we are in, and a fire has started. It's moving very quickly from the upper floor down to where I am. I have to get out of here. I'm gagging from the smoke, and the flames have raced through the entire house. Charles just ran back into the room I am in, but the flames were in his way. He made his way over to the table. I think he wants that knife he left behind."

"Please continue, Lila."

"The house I'm in is very old. It must have been abandoned many years ago. All of the windows are broken and I just heard a huge crash. As Charles was reaching for the knife, one of the large ceiling beams cracked and collapsed on him. Oh, my God, I can see his head bleeding and he's not moving. I have to get out. Please someone help me. Please."

"Lila, I want you to relax for a moment. Can you do that for me?" the doctor asked.

"Please help me. The fire is so close now. I can feel the

searing heat on my legs and face."

"Lila, I would like you to take a deep breath now and just listen to my voice as I guide you back. You're in a safe and very peaceful place now, and I'm going to count back from five to one. When I reach one, you'll be able to open your eyes and feel totally refreshed. Five, four, three, two, and one. You can open your eyes now.

"How are you feeling, Laura?" Dr. Morrissey asked.

"Honestly, I'm not quite sure. For a moment, I felt like I was involved with some type of fire in an old building, but I can't seem to remember much else."

"Well. Laura, you were reliving a very emotional event. It seems this man, Charles, kidnapped you and took you to an old house. There seemed to be a very bad storm taking place and the house was struck by lightning. A large fire ensued and we got to the point where a large ceiling beam collapsed and apparently struck Charles, killing him."

"You know, Dr. Morrissey, I would never have believed any of this until I began going through those old news articles. It's just incredibly freaky that I have this ability actually to relive someone else's life using this technique."

"Well, Laura, I think we might actually get to the bottom of your phobia with just one more session. Are you game?" the doctor asked.

"Without a doubt, Doctor, I'm ready. I have to know what happened."

"Great, Laura. Let's meet again at the same time next week."

Chapter 41

After finishing up with Dr. Morrissey, I decided to head up to Central Park. Fall in New York City is special. Special because Central Park has the largest concentration of trees anywhere in the city, and just taking in the invigorating brisk autumn air along with the fantastic colors in the trees is a site to behold. As a lifelong resident of the city, I had never taken one of those horse carriage rides, and today would be perfect just to take in the sights and sounds of the *city that never sleeps*.

I paid my fare to one of the horsemen and off we went. I can't think of another place in the world where one can see so magnificent a skyline. Oh, maybe Paris, but New York, at least at this time of year, was even more special. As my ride continued, I sat back and took it all in. The varying colors and hues of the parks autumn leaves were at their peak. As I listened to the sound of the horse's shoes making contact with the pavement, I thought back to a simpler time in America, a time where many used horses as their only transportation.

We passed the Metropolitan Museum, and it was then that fragments of today's session began to replay in my mind. I couldn't even begin to imagine what that poor girl, Lila, was going through. First she's kidnapped, then watches this nut case, Charles, get creamed when parts of the house fall in on him while Lila is burning to death. At least that was the account that I had found in one of the Atlanta newspapers. But the question I had kept asking myself was how all of this had tied in with this phobia I had about singing.

Ever since I was a child, just the thought of singing has made me shut down mentally. I would always feel my throat closing, which would then lead to a mild panic attack. How did this possibly relate to my situation? I guess I'll get my answer during the next session with Dr. Morrissey. So until then, perhaps it will just have to remain a mystery.

After my ride was over, I tipped the horseman and then called Beth on my cell phone. "You ready for the next installment?" I asked.

"I can't wait to hear all the gory details. Where would you like to meet?" Beth asked.

"Well, I'm on Columbus Circle," I said. "How about we get a late lunch at *Per Se*? You know where that is, don't you?"

"I sure do. Start walking and I'll be there before you get to the front door."

I had to walk several blocks to get to the restaurant, and sure enough, good old Beth was never one to disappoint. There she was in a gorgeous grey wool coat, a colorful scarf, and her signature sunglasses. At times I have wondered about my friend, but as crazy as she was, she was one of the best friends I had.

"So, My Dear, would you like to hear what happened today?" I asked Beth.

"Wild horses couldn't keep me away. Let's go inside," she said.

After we were seated, we ordered a couple of Manhattans and I began to tell Beth what had transpired at my last session. As I rattled off detail after detail, I noticed Beth was hanging on to my every word. She never interrupted me once, and just took it all in.

"So, what do you think, Old Girl?" I asked.

"I think this would make a fantastic book. I mean, shit like this doesn't happen every day in someone's life, Laura. This is just amazing. On top of everything else, you actually found documents to back up this insane story. What did the doctor think of the news clippings?"

"It just further verified this particular form of psychiatry, Beth. There really is something to these past-life regressions, and the doctor feels that during the next session, I might just have the answer I was looking for when I originally went to see him."

"Oh, you mean the singing thing, right?"

"Yes, Dear. The singing thing," I replied.

"This is really amazing, Laura. I can't wait to hear the final outcome. And that poor girl being burned alive must have been a terrible thing to experience. But at least as far as you know, this creep, Charles, bought the farm that evening. Correct?"

"It sure seems that way, and honestly, I'm not sure just how much more of this story there actually is," I said.

"You know, Laura, at this point I think I'll just have a house salad. My stomach is in knots just thinking about this creepy stuff," Beth said.

"Me too, Beth. I think I'll do the same, and just keep it on the light side."

We finished eating and as we left the restaurant, I told Beth I was going to make it an early night again as these sessions seemed so exhausting.

“Do what you have to do, Girlfriend. We'll talk soon,” Beth said.

And with that, we parted company. The days were getting shorter and it was nearly dark by the time I had reached my apartment. After I walked in, I got comfortable and decided to lie down on the couch and just close my eyes for a while. I didn't realize just how much it could take out of someone going through these gut-wrenching sessions.

As I felt myself drifting off, I suddenly was startled when the stereo began playing. At first I thought it was my imagination, but it wasn't. Then I felt that presence as I did at the foot of my bed the week before. I had almost fallen asleep, and when the stereo came on by itself, it was playing that same tune, *Blue Skies*. How could this be? Was this some message from the departed? Was there supposed to be some trail I was supposed to follow? Something just wasn't right, and this time I just grabbed the plug for the stereo and pulled it out of the wall socket. Now if the damned thing played again, I was going to go apartment hunting for a new home.

Chapter 42

Given the information that had come out of my last regression session from this morning, this had to be one of my more exciting days. The salad I had with Beth at lunchtime was about all I cared to eat. I was just exhausted, both physically and mentally, and was looking forward to a good night's sleep. It was getting close to eight p.m., and I was nursing a Scotch-and-water while I sat at my desk going over some of the newer clippings that I had found at the library the day before. How terrible it must have been for that young girl, Lila, to have gone through the events that she did and then eventually lose her life because of Charles.

I've often wondered if this was how the universe tries to balance itself out between good and evil. Yet it did seem a shame that Lila had to suffer as she did. At least some positive identification could be made when Lila's mother recognized the pattern on her daughters dress—or what was left of it after the fire. As I sat reviewing some of the reports, I decided to jump on my computer and read about the life and times of people that had lived through the Great Depression. Site after site painted such a dismal picture of life in America during that period. Men of means, having lost everything, would turn to alcoholism and/or become drifters, such as those that rode the rails to parts unknown, including Atlanta. Others committed suicide, and families were left broken. No wonder they called it the Great

Depression.

How much more depressing could it get just reading about that time in our country's history? I finally had my fill and decided to get some sleep. At least I had the day off tomorrow and it would be as good a time as any to catch up on some house cleaning and trying to balance my checkbook.

As hard as I tried, I couldn't fall asleep. My brain was locked onto hearing those terrible screams from Lila as she was literally burning to death. I needed a diversion, or at least something that would put me out for the night. I turned on one of the late shows, and then proceeded to pop a Xanax, thinking that surely that would put me in a drowsy state, especially with the Scotch I had been sipping.

Sure enough, in about half an hour, my eyes began to get very heavy. So this was as good a time as any to get some much needed sleep. I crawled into bed, pulled up the covers. and proceeded to pass out. I didn't even set the alarm clock. The world could have come to an end and I just didn't care. Tomorrow would be a new day, and at least it would bring me one day closer to my next appointment with Dr. Morrissey.

Chapter 43

As night passed into a new day, it was time to get up and get my day going. After getting out of bed, I opened the curtains in the bedroom to check on the weather. As I stared out the window, I was fascinated, as always, by the different colors and hues the city landscape could take on depending on the weather. On sunny days, buildings with their steel and glass facades glistened and sparkled, creating a cityscape that seemed to vibrate with energy. But today it was raining, and the city seemed dismal and gloomy as it displayed somber shades of grey.

Something else that always interested me was watching people on the streets down below. I was on the forty-third floor of my building, and if I let my eyes go out of focus just briefly, pedestrians below looked like ants scurrying around. All with a mission going from point A to point B. The city seemed to be a well-oiled machine, with all those people below heading in a thousand different directions. Yet, at the end of the day, it all seemed to make sense.

Well, I thought to myself, *I can watch city life all day, or have something for breakfast.* So I opted for breakfast. After I got that out of the way, I changed into a pair of sweat pants and my ratty old college sweat shirt. It was time to tackle those dust bunnies that had this curious habit of occupying every corner of my apartment.

As I was cleaning, I thought I was losing my mind when

the freaking stereo turned on again. How could this be? I walked over to it and bent down to see if I might have plugged it back in. No, the plug was still on the floor where I had left it. *How is this possible?* I thought. *This doesn't make any sense.* I called down to the superintendent of our building and asked if he could come up and check the wiring in my apartment. He must have thought I was crazy, but he arrived in just a few minutes.

"Good morning, Laura," Jim said. "What seems to be the problem?"

"Jim, can you take a look at my stereo system? For some reason, it just seems to turn on by itself. Take a look at the plug, Jim. It's on the floor, and yet it's playing. That's impossible, isn't it?" I asked.

"Wow, Laura! This is some fancy setup you have here. Do you happen to still have the operating instructions around?" he asked.

"Sure, Jim. They're in my desk."

I walked over to the desk and handed the instructions to Jim, and after about five minutes of reading, a broad smile came across his face.

"What's so funny?" I asked Jim.

"Well, Laura, this unit came with a backup battery system, so that if the power ever goes out, you can still listen to the radio. It's pretty much like the newer alarm clocks. If the power goes out, the clock will keep working, usually for another twelve hours on battery backup. See this little switch right on the side of the unit? If you ever want to shut the battery backup off, just flip it and it will shut off."

"Well I'll be!" I said. "I never knew that about this system. I thought I was losing it, but this makes sense."

"Anything to help," Jim said. "By the way, Laura, electricians have been working on wiring in the building. So if the power gets cut off, your stereo will turn on. Is there anything else I might be able to do for you while I'm here?"

"No, Jim. You've been a great help in solving this mystery for me."

I smiled at Jim and thanked him for coming up on such short notice, and he was gone as fast as he had arrived.

After that mystery was solved, I got back into cleaning. The bathroom was next on my to-do list. I took care of the shower and toilet, as well as the sink and mirrors, and then it happened again. This was the third time I felt the presence of someone or something watching me. I walked out of the bathroom into my bedroom, and no one was there. I then headed to the living room and then the kitchen and still nothing.

As I was walking back to the bathroom to finish up, I passed a hallway mirror and stopped dead in my tracks. As I turned to look into the mirror, there she was. It had to be her. She had flowing auburn hair and must have been in her mid-twenties and wearing what appeared to be the dress that was described in the police report, a white dress with faded yellow roses. She didn't move at all, and all I could feel was my heart getting ready to pound out of my chest. As crazy and frightening as the image was, I tried to utter the name, *Lila.*

"Are you Lila?" I asked." At that moment the image in the mirror was consumed by flames and in an instant, it had disappeared.

Suddenly I felt the blood literally draining out of my head. I must have passed out from the shock of seeing that image, because the next thing I remember was when I opened my eyes and found myself on the floor, and scared totally shitless. I had to call Dr. Morrissey and let him know what had just happened.

Chapter 44

Life at times seems like a sick joke or a bad dream. As I opened my eyes, all I could see was a bright light over my head. Where was I? I'm flat on my back lying on some type of stretcher. Why are my arms wrapped around me like some embalmed mummy? Why are there straps holding me down? I screamed out, "Where am I?"

A large black man that was dressed in white came over to me and said, "Relax, Susan. You're in safe hands. No one is going to hurt you." His nametag said his name was *Horace.*

"I know you, Horace, but you're supposed to be a white man. Don't you run the Five and Dime anymore, Horace?" I asked.

Horace looked to the other side of the stretcher I was on and said to a woman who also was dressed in white, "I think we should give her that shot now. The doctor will be here as soon as he finishes talking to her parents."

I watched this woman, who was probably a nurse, as she injected something into an IV line that was in my arm. "Who are you?" I asked. "Do I know you?"

"Why of course you do, Susan. My name is Beth, and I'm the head nurse on your floor."

"My floor? Where?" I asked. "Where am I?"

"Susan, Dr. Morrissey is just talking to your parents now. He will be here in a few minutes," Beth said.

My mind began to race with images that seemed to play backwards at light speed. All I knew was that I was being held down on a stretcher and this woman, Beth, had just injected me with something. *I'm getting so drowsy. I want to see Momma.* And that was the last thing I remember thinking. Where was Momma?

As my eyes closed, I heard Beth say, "Horace, stay here with Susan while I go and get the doctor. I believe he's in his office with Susan's parents."

*****

"Welcome back, Olivia. How are you doing, Oscar? Please have a seat and we can discuss your daughter's case," I suggested to Susan's parents.

"Honestly, Dr. Morrissey," Olivia said, "Susan has been here at Wyckoff Sanitarium for nearly fifteen years, and my husband and I have been hoping against hope that she would have made some progress by now."

"As you know, Olivia," I began, "Susan suffers from schizophrenia, and medical science has established that this is a condition which the vast majority of schizophrenic patients are born with. Unfortunately, it usually doesn't manifest until adolescence or the early twenties in men, and usually in the thirties in women.

"We also have been trying to deal with Susan's multiple personality disorder, which we all realize is quite severe. A person with MPD may develop as many as 100 personalities, but the average is 10. She may take on alternate personalities of the same sex, a different sex, or both sexes at the same time. Sometimes an MPD patient even takes on the physical characteristics of her different personalities, such as a certain way of walking or moving, or even talking. Additionally, depression and self-mutilation are common. We have to keep her heavily medicated. As you know, she's attempted suicide several times while here."

"Dr. Morrissey," Oscar began, "as you know, this was a difficult decision for Susan's mother and me, having to place her here at Wyckoff. But it just seems that after years of treatment, our daughter hasn't made much in the way of progress."

"I can certainly understand how both of you must feel, but at this point, it's her personal safety that we're concerned about," I explained to Susan's parents. "Treatment is mainly psychotherapy with hypnosis, and we have made some progress with Susan's MPD. The goal is to deconstruct the different personalities and unite them into one. Where we seem to be having the greatest problem is in getting the schizophrenia under control. At times, Susan becomes quite violent. She has just been mildly sedated, so if you would like to see her, you can talk to her in the treatment room now," the doctor said.

"I'm not sure I can take much more of this, Oscar," Olivia said.

"Take it easy, Olivia," Oscar consoled. "We know Susan is in the best of hands. I know we feel helpless in dealing with this, but as her father, I want the best care she can get, and I know you do, too."

Chapter 45

After finishing our discussion in my office, I walked down the hall with Susan's parents to the treatment room. As a father as well as a doctor, I knew that Susan's parents were genuinely concerned about their daughter. In my thirty-five years of practice, I had never seen a case as severe as Susan's; but where there is life, there is always hope. As we walked into a room adjacent to the treatment room, Susan's parents were able to see their daughter through a one-way mirror. She had been mildly sedated, but would still be able to converse with her parents. The only question was whether the conversation would be even remotely intelligible.

As Susan's parents watched their daughter, the anguish on their faces was unmistakable. "Would you like to go in and talk with her?" I asked.

"Yes," Olivia said. "Oscar, do you want to come in with me?"

"Yes, Olivia, of course. Maybe today will be different from all the other times we've been here."

Both parents walked into the treatment room and stood at their daughter's side. "Susan, it's Mom and Dad," Olivia said. "Susan, can you hear me?"

"Momma, Momma, is that you?" Susan began. "Oh Momma, I feel so bad that I couldn't do more. I know we really needed the money but when Peter was murdered, my whole world came to an end," Susan replied.

Olivia looked at me and asked, "Is this normal for someone with MPD, Dr. Morrissey?" This was one of the few times that Susan was actually in character, talking with a southern accent.

"Yes, Olivia, it happens from time to time," I replied.

"Remember me, Susan? It's Dad."

"Oh no, you're not my father. You're Oscar, that cook at the Five and Dime. Don't you remember? You made me that bologna sandwich with the really sour pickle."

Oscar looked away in frustration, and no doubt Olivia felt equally let down that their daughter hadn't seemed to be making any progress. Oscar leaned down and gave his daughter a kiss on her forehead, while Olivia was obviously on the verge of tears. It was best at this point just to escort both of them out of the room, and I suggested we return to my office.

"Please have a seat. I know this has been difficult for both of you, but please bear in mind that as long as Susan is here, at least she can be kept safe. Every day new medications are being made available and new technologies are being developed. I'm quite confident that at some point we will be able to stabilize Susan so that she may function as normally as possible."

"Dr. Morrissey," Olivia asked, "exactly what do you consider *functioning normally* to be?"

"At best, Susan will be integrated slowly into the rest of the patient population. At worst, she may spend the rest of her life in the isolation room where she currently resides."

"I want her receiving the best care possible," Oscar declared. "I want nothing but the best for our Susan."

"Susan is receiving the best and most current care available today, Oscar, and I will do everything in my power in trying to get Susan to a point where she is far more stabilized than she is now. There are never any guarantees, but with perseverance, I do believe, in my professional opinion, that we can make progress."

"We'll be back again in another month, Dr. Morrissey," Oscar said, "and hopefully we'll see something in the way of a positive change by then."

"That's what we're working for, Oscar. I will have one of the orderlies escort you off the floor and back to the main entrance, as I do have rounds to make at the moment."

"Thank you, Dr. Morrissey," Olivia said. "We'll see you again in a month."

It wasn't long after Susan's parents left the building that I returned to her treatment room. I asked Horace and Beth to help her off the stretcher and into a comfortable chair.

"Beth," I said, "I should be back in just a few minutes and we'll start the hypnosis session. But first I have to catch up with several residents and finish morning rounds. I'll be back in about fifteen minutes."

Chapter 46

My best friend, Beth, along with Horace from the Five and Dime, sat me up, and Horace swung my legs over the side of the stretcher.

"Are we going on a trip, Horace?" I asked.

"No, Susan, we're just going to have a seat over here and wait for Dr. Morrissey to come back."

"Why do you keep calling me Susan, Horace? You know my real name is Lila. Peter! Where is Peter?"

"Susan, just try to relax for a few minutes and the doctor will be back to start your session," Beth said."

"I know I don't belong here, Beth," I said. "You surely are making a mistake in keeping me here at the police station. Can't you see I don't belong here? I know Momma would be mad as the dickens if she knew how you were treating me, having me all tied up and such. Horace, where is that new umbrella you gave me? I can't seem to find it anywhere?"

"She's such a beautiful woman, Horace," I heard Beth say. Who was she talking about? Then Beth continued, "It's a shame that she's spent nearly fifteen years here and yet seems to have made such little progress."

"How could some poor soul remain at the police station for 15 years?" I asked. But they ignored me, and kept right on talking.

"I know, Beth," Horace replied. "We've seen so many patients over the years and so many were able to be helped, and yet Susan seems forever lost with multiple personalities. You would think that after all these years that greater progress would have been made in cases like this. I can only imagine what must go through a patient's mind. Do you think they feel lost or trapped in some way, Beth?"

"It's hard to tell, Horace. Sometimes you get the feeling that some of the patients don't have any idea who or where they are, and yet at other times they can seem very lucid. Just stay with Susan, Horace. I have to give an injection to the patient in room 404. I'll be back in just a couple of minutes."

"Sure, Beth, no problem," Horace said.

As Beth left the room, Dr. Morrissey was just coming back into the treatment room. Horace sat in a chair in the corner and the doctor sat next to me. "How are you feeling today, Susan?" the doctor asked.

"I don't know where Susan is, but I'm her best friend, Lila. Are we going to Peter's funeral today?" I asked.

"No, not today, Lila," the doctor said. "I want you to listen to my voice and follow the instructions I'm going to give you. First, Lila, just close your eyes and think of a peaceful, wonderful place where you don't have a care in the world. Can you do that for me, Lila?"

As the doctor kept talking to me, I felt myself drifting away as if I were floating in space and out of my physical body. The doctor told me to relax and count back from five to one. When I said the word *one*, I would be in a deep state of relaxation.

"Can you still hear my voice, Lila?" the doctor asked.

"Yes, I can hear you, but I have to go."

"Where do you have to go, Lila?"

"I have to get out of this place. The house is on fire and I'm tied to a chair. I can't breathe and I'm choking from the smoke. That bad man, Charles, is over there, but I think he's dead. I just know he killed Peter. I just know it."

"Try to relax, Lila. What happens after the fire in the house?" the doctor asked.

"I feel the heat from the flames. My skin is starting to blister from the intense heat I feel all over my body. I'm choking from all of the smoke, and burning embers are dancing through the air and falling on my pretty Sunday dress. It's beginning to burn and I feel deep pain. I'm trying to take one last breath while my skin feels like a thousand needles are sticking me."

"Can you feel anything else, Lila?" the doctor asked.

"No. Now I feel nothing because I'm disconnected from my body. I'm floating above the dead girl in the chair and now I have to leave this place. I'm going to meet Peter. I know he is waiting for me."

"Lila, the doctor said, can you tell me if you see your momma?"

"No. Momma isn't here. But Mr. Gibbons is here; he's standing over yonder talking to old Judge Johnston."

"Can you see anyone else, Lila?"

"No. It's getting dark now. Everyone is leaving me and I'm all alone standing in emptiness. There is a mist rising from the floor and as I watch it, it is creeping up on me and surrounding me. I keep hearing a voice that says, *Come with me.*"

"Lila, can you tell me anything else about this mist?"

"It's so cool against my skin and it's getting very thick as it covers my entire body. Wait. Now the mist is dropping back to the floor, but as it lowers around me, I'm fading. I just seem to be fading away as if this mist or fog is sucking out any of my existence. I can't see my arms or the rest of my body. But I know I am here. Yes, I know I am here, but not in physical form any longer."

"Susan, I want you to take in a deep breath and listen to my voice. I will count backwards from five to one. When I reach *one*, you'll be able to open your eyes, and Lila will never come back to visit you again. She doesn't have to because she is at peace. Do you understand what I have said, Susan?"

"Yes, I understand."

"Susan, I'm counting back from five now; five, four, three, two, one. You can open your eyes now. How are you feeling, Susan?"

"I looked up to the man that was talking to me. I know I had seen him many times before. "Are you here to help me? Are you a doctor?" I asked.

"Yes, Susan, I'm here to help you."

Was this really a doctor? How was he going to help me? Then I heard him say to Beth, "Can you and Horace help Susan back onto the stretcher and wheel her back to her room. Make sure you keep the restraints on, Horace. I'm sure you haven't forgotten what happened the last time she attacked you."

"Yes, Dr. Morrissey. The restraints will be kept on. You can rest assured of that," Horace said.

Then the doctor told Beth he had dictation to do in his office, and left the room.

Chapter 47

After Dr. Morrissey left my treatment room, Horace began pushing my stretcher down a very long hallway. Lying on my back, all I could see was one ceiling light after another passing above me. Maybe the injection I was given just calmed me down, but I felt so at peace. I'm glad that Olivia and Oscar took the time off from the Five and Dime to see me today. I just feel so bad about that poor young man that was murdered.

As the stretcher came to a stop, Horace asked me if I felt I could get up off the stretcher and stand.

"Yes, I think I can, Horace. Are we back home now? Is Momma here?" I asked.

"Yes, we're back home, but I'm afraid that Momma isn't here. I'll walk you into your room, but I'm going to have to keep the restraints on you and tie them down to the bed."

"Do what you must, Horace. I'm going to sing with Momma later," I said.

Horace took hold of my arm and helped me to sit up. Then he helped me off the stretcher and walked me into the small room in my house. I knew Momma would be here soon and I wanted to be ready for her.

"Horace, where is my dress? You know the one with the pretty yellow roses on it?"

"I'm not quite sure. I'll have to go look for it," Horace

said. Then he helped me to my bed and began to tie the straps on the white jacket I was wearing to the four corners of my bed.

"Horace, you just have to find that dress of mine. I think Momma is going to be here any minute."

"Don't you worry, Lila. I promise I will look for it. Are you comfortable now, Lila?" Horace asked.

"Yes, Horace. I'll just wait here for Momma to come to see me," I said.

As I looked out of my window I wondered again why Momma felt it was necessary to have bars placed in the window. I would have to ask her when she got here, because I had never understood why.

It must be getting later in the day, I thought. *The sky and clouds have taken on a purple hue, just as the sun is getting ready to set. I know Momma will be here soon.*

Chapter 48

I waited for what seemed ages, and Momma still hadn't arrived. Horace had brought my dinner earlier and he was kind enough to get me out of my bed and let me sit in a chair so I could eat. He said he would be back later to help me back into my bed. I can't rightly understand why I am in this place. This isn't my home. I know Momma must be mad at me because of all the laundry that must be piling up.

Everything is white here in this place; the ceiling, the floor, and the walls—everything is white. I swear I never have been in a place like this. I can't imagine why they put what looks like mattresses on the walls. If it were me, I would take them down and replace them with pretty pictures of flowers. I always loved flowers, especially those yellow roses that smelled so sweet in the late spring.

I hear someone outside my door. "Is that you, Momma?" I called out.

The handle on my door began to turn and then the door opened. "Who are you?" I asked.

"You know who I am, Lila, don't you? I'm Charles. I'm the man that stood outside your window while you would sing. I asked you to stop singing that song, *Blue Skies*, but you just kept on singing it, didn't you?"

"I once knew a man named Charles, but I don't think you're him," I said.

"It's me all right, Lila," Charles said, "and I have come back to take you with me."

"Where do you want to take me, Charles?" I asked.

"We're going to a place you know very well. I came back to see you, Lila, because there is something I still have left to do. You see, Lila, you got off lucky. You only burned to death; you didn't die by my hand."

At that moment, my heart began to race as I felt beads of sweat forming on my forehead. I tried to get loose from the straps that held me down on the chair I was sitting on, but I couldn't break free. The harder I tried to escape from this man, Charles, the more panicked I became.

*****

"What the hell was that scream, Horace?" Beth asked. me.

"It sounds like it came from Susan's room," I said.

"You'd better go take a look, Horace. Is Susan still strapped into her chair?" Beth asked.

"Yes, Beth. I strapped her up in her chair for dinner and was going to place her back in bed for the evening. Let me just grab the master key and I'll go and check on her," I told Beth.

"Horace, I'll be right behind you with 5 cc's of Diazepam. You'd better hurry, Horace," Beth said.

The screams were getting louder and louder. Even Dr. Morrissey heard them and came onto the patient's floor. As I opened the door to Susan's room, all I saw was a woman whose very facial features seemed to change before my eyes. I was just an orderly, but thank goodness Beth was right behind me with Susan's sedation. As Beth walked into the room, I asked her if she could help me untie the straps holding Susan in her day chair.

"Hold on, Horace, and let me give her this shot first. She'll be more manageable then, Beth said."

After a brief struggle, Beth was able to inject the sedative into Susan's IV At least it allowed the medication to work a lot faster. At that moment, Dr. Morrissey walked into Susan's room and helped us get her back into her bed, while I took care of tying Susan's restraints down.

*****

"Thank you for your help," I told Horace. "Beth, I think she's under control now. I'm going to stay with her for a few minutes, so you both can leave now if you like. Thanks to both of you."

As the injection was taking effect, I drew Susan's chair to the side of her bed. "Susan, can you hear me?" I asked.

"I was all alone until that man came into my room."

"What man was that, Susan?"

"Why do you keep calling me Susan? My name is Lila."

"All right, Lila. Who was the man that upset you so much?"

"It was that man, Charles. He wanted to take me with him."

"Where did he want to take you, Lila?" I asked.

"I'm not sure, but I know he was fixing to hurt me."

"Lila, do you know where you are at this moment?"

"Why, I'm in my home and I'm waiting for Momma to arrive so I can sing while she plays the piano."

Even in the most hopeless of cases, I still believed, as a physician, I had to do all I could in somehow bringing Susan back to some state of reality.

"Is there anything I can do for you, Lila?"

"No sir. I'm alone now, and I'm not sure I will ever see Momma again. All I have ever been is alone."

It was getting rather late and I still had dictation on a couple of cases left. At times I had thought that Susan was progressing, as she did have those rare lucid moments. But then she would always relapse. The medical profession has made great strides in treating mental illness, and I wasn't going to give up on Susan now.

"I think you're going to be just fine, Lila," I said. "Why don't you just try to get some sleep and I'll see you in the morning."

I got up from the chair and placed it back against the far wall. Tomorrow would be another day.

Chapter 49

"Good morning, Horace," Beth greeted me as I walked in.
"Good morning, Beth. How has the day been going so far?"

"It's been pretty quiet except for Susan," Beth told me. According to the night nurse's notes, she had a very restless night. She apparently was highly delusional and kept screaming that there was a man in her room that was going to take her away to a bad place. Finally, they sedated her again and she seems fairly quiet now. I'm just waiting for the doctor to get here as I wanted to know if we should adjust her medication schedule."

"Sounds like it was a rough night," I said.

"Nights always seem to be difficult for many of these patients," Beth said. "If I didn't know Susan's background, I actually would start believing that there really is someone named Charles that she keeps ranting about.

"Oh, there's Dr. Morrissey. I'd better bring him up to date on Susan's condition."

*****

I walked over to the nurse's station and picked up Susan's chart.

"Another difficult night, I see," I said to Beth.

"I'm afraid so, Doctor. Susan seems so fixated on this man, Charles, and I have to wonder sometimes if there was actually a man in her life at some point before coming here, who might have had that name?"

"I have a hunch about that, Beth, that I would like to follow up on. In fact, I'm going to be out of the office for several hours today to do just that. I'll stop in and see Susan before I leave."

I brought Susan's chart with me and proceeded down the hall toward her room. As I approached, I heard Susan singing that song, *Blue Skies,* that she always mentions. As I walked into Susan's room, she was still strapped down to her bed.

"Good morning, Susan. How are we feeling this morning?" I asked.

"You left me alone and that evil man, Charles, kept visiting me. He told me he was going to take me away, but I kept telling him that I had to wait for Momma to arrive—but she never did."

Susan, do you know who this man, Charles, really is? Where do you know him from?" I asked.

"Charles must surely be the devil. I just know he killed that young man, Peter. Then one rainy night he came after me."

"But why would he want to hurt you?" I asked.

"Because he never wanted me to sing that song, *Blue Skies*," she said.

"I see, Susan."

As Susan continued to ramble on, I was reviewing the charge nurses notes from the evening before. Susan just wasn't making any significant progress.

"Susan, I'll stop in a little later today and we can talk a little longer, okay?"

Susan never answered and simply went catatonic, staring out her window. At least the medication given her earlier seemed to keep her somewhat calmer than usual.

I left Susan's room, and while walking back to my office, a thought occurred to me. I knew it probably was a long shot, but I was determined to find out whether any of Susan's mental excursions in her mind about events in the Deep South back in 1933 had any merit at all. It was probably a waste of time, but at least there would be one more thing to cross off my list as possible triggers for Susan's violent outbreaks.

Chapter 50

After returning to my office, I called up a good friend who was an attorney. I figured he might be able to lead me in the right direction when looking for specific information regarding past events.

"Jack? Hi, it's Dave Morrissey, and I need to pick your brain, if that's okay."

"Sure. Shoot, Dave," Jack replied.

"Jack, I have a patient who suffers from Multiple Personality Disorder, and I'm really hitting a brick wall with this patient."

"Well, how can I help you, Dave?" Jack asked.

"This patient seems to have an extraordinary recall of events that have taken place over eighty years ago, and on a lark, I wondered where I might be able to dig up information about a certain time period in American history."

"What particular time period are you talking about, Dave?" Jack asked.

"It was the summer of 1933, in Atlanta, Georgia," I replied.

"That shouldn't be too difficult, Dave. Just head down to the main branch of the New York Public Library. They have a very extensive collection of microfilm files from old newspapers. So if you're looking for something factual, I think that would be your best shot."

"Thanks, Jack. I never thought about the library. I'll

check into it. By the way, how are Mary and the kids?" I asked.

"Everyone is just fine, Dave. Thanks for asking." "

Thanks again, Jack. Sounds like I have my work cut out for me. Talk to you soon."

After hanging up with Jack, I cleared my calendar for the rest of the day and decided to drive into the city. There had to be some connection to the events that Susan kept talking about, yet how was it possible for a woman that was born decades after this alleged event that took place have any information about it? Especially since she has been at Wyckoff for the better part of fifteen years?

I put my coat on, and braced myself for the cooler weather, as autumn would soon turn to winter. I stopped at the nurse's station and told Beth that I would be gone for most of the day, but would see her before her shift ended. It only took about forty-five minutes to get into the city, and after parking the car, I made my way to the Forty-Second Street branch of the main library.

I asked one of the library attendants where I might find the microfilm section, and he pointed me in the right direction. After doing a search, I found several old newspapers that were in circulation in Atlanta in 1933. On a whim, I put the name *Lila Hartley* into the search engine, and within seconds I had found what I had been looking for. But this was impossible.

I read of the murder of a judge's son, one Peter Johnston, in August of 1933, along with the name of a young girl that had accompanied him to the movies, Miss. Lila Hartley. The young man died almost instantly after his throat was slashed, according to the police report, but as I continued to follow the story, it became even more bizarre.

As it turned out, approximately one month later, two bodies were found after a house fire. One of the deceased was identified as Charles Sycamore, a stockbroker who had lost everything in the stock market crash of 1929. Another body found tied to a chair and burned beyond recognition was that of a young woman. A part of a dress was found near the body and it seems the mother of the young girl was able to identify the pattern of the dress her daughter, Lila, had owned.

As I sat taking copious notes, I couldn't believe that Susan possibly could have known all of these facts about something that had happened back in the 1930's. Could she possibly have stumbled across this story in the past? This didn't make any sense, and yet there it was in black and white. After I finished, I just sat in my seat and thought to myself that no one in his right mind would ever believe this story.

Chapter 51

I gathered my notes, left the library, and headed back to the hospital. I knew I was as sane as anyone, but Jesus, how in the world could Susan possibly have latched on to this information that ultimately became one of her alternative personalities? Thankfully traffic was pretty light heading out of the city, and I made it back to Wyckoff in record time.

When I got to my office I began to compare the information from the news accounts with statements Susan had made over the years. Everything checked out, right down to the description of Lila's run-down row house. I thought to myself, *This is just impossible*, but I knew if I lived to be a hundred, I never would get a straight answer out of Susan. My only hope was in trying to question Olivia and Oscar, Susan's parents. Perhaps they might be able to shed some light on this story.

I went through Susan's contact information and gave Susan's parents a call. Olivia picked up.

"Good evening Olivia, its Dr. Morrissey."

"Is everything all right with Susan?" she asked.

"Yes, Olivia. Susan is fine. The reason I'm calling is because I came across some information regarding her case, and wondered if any of this might sound familiar to you."

"Such as what?" Olivia asked.

"Olivia, do you or Oscar have any family that has ever

lived in the state of Georgia, or any who currently live there?" I asked.

"No, Doctor. Our family actually originated from New England and New York. We don't even have relatives that ever lived in the south. Have you discovered something, Dr. Morrissey, that might help Susan?"

"Honestly, Olivia, I'm not sure. I just thought it might be worth a shot in trying to unravel why Susan has taken on the life of the Lila girl, and why she seems so scared of someone named Charles. Thanks for your time, Olivia. If something comes up, I will be in touch. Have a good evening and we'll talk soon."

Another dead-end. And then it happened—a bloodcurdling scream from Susan's room. I left the office and rushed onto the patient's floor where Beth and Horace, along with two other orderlies, were running in the direction of her room.

The screams continued, and were ear-piercing. Susan kept saying over and over, "Charles is going to take me away. He's going to kill me. He's coming to get me. Momma, I need you."

"Beth" I said, "give her five cc's of klonopin.

Finally, after the injection, Susan began to quiet down.

"Beth, keep her strapped to the bed. I don't want Susan hurting herself."

"Yes, of course, Dr. Morrissey," Beth said.

It had been a long day for me, and after dealing with Susan's screams, I still was totally bewildered in trying to make sense of what was happening with this her. I had just returned to my office when Beth knocked on my office door.

"How can I help you, Beth?" I asked.

"Susan seems to be having these psychotic outbreaks more often, Dr. Morrissey. I hate having to keep her in restraints all day and night. I just wondered if there is possibly any other way to handle the situation. On the other hand, I suppose the restraints are best for now."

"Beth, I'm going to share something with you that I came across today."

"Oh, what is that, Dr. Morrissey?" Beth asked.

"I took a drive into the city today and went to the main branch of the public library. I did a little searching based on some of the events and timeline that Susan is always talking about. To my surprise, I found articles about the death of a young man that Lila—I mean Susan—keeps referring to. What she is talking about actually happened."

"What actually happened, Doctor?"

"There really was a murder in the summer of 1933 in Atlanta. A young man, the son of a local judge, was murdered, just as Susan has been saying. Roughly a month later, two people were found dead in a house fire. One was a man identified as Charles Sycamore. Does that name mean anything to you, Beth?

"No, not at all. How about you?"

"Well, it just occurred to me that I once had some dealings with a doctor by that name. But the guy who died in the fire was a stockbroker from more than 80 years ago, so I suppose it is just a coincidence. The other body was that of a young woman. The only possible ID of the girl was from the remnants of a dress identified by Lila's mother as her Sunday dress—the one Susan keeps talking about.

"Are you kidding me, Dr. Morrissey? These delusional stories coming from Susan are actually based on fact? How could she possible know about them?" Beth asked.

"That's the difficult part, Beth. Susan isn't stable enough for us to find out. This is like working a puzzle from opposite ends and trying to meet up in the middle. This could take years to unravel."

"I don't envy your task, Dr. Morrissey. Such a sad case!"

"Beth, I think I'm going to call it night and head home. I have a lot of thinking to do. Your shift relief should be here soon. I know these 12-hour shifts can drag. I'll see you in the morning."

"Good night, Doctor. I'll be here bright and early," Beth smiled.

Chapter 52

As I got into my car in the hospital parking lot, I just sat for a moment thinking about the information I had come across at the library. There had to be some logical series of events that had come into Susan's life that would have caused her to latch on to this very real story about the girl, Lila. But how? That was the question that kept driving me crazy.

When I arrived home, I poured myself a vodka and tonic and sat down at my desk to go over the articles I had copied earlier from the library. As I sat at my desk, I kept looking for some connection that Susan might have made, but for the life of me, I couldn't establish one. This case by far had to be one of the most fascinating I had ever come across. I could only imagine the very real fear that Susan must have felt as she believed that this man, Charles, was going to come back from the grave to take her.

I just didn't have the answers I was looking for. I just couldn't connect the events of eighty-plus years ago with a woman who neither had relatives in the south, nor to the best of my knowledge, had ever spent any time in Atlanta. I was almost tempted to call a number of colleagues and set up a round-table discussion about this case, which seemed as complicated as a Gordian knot. I was at a complete loss. To make it worse, Lila was only one of Susan's imaginary people. Where does one begin to unravel this psychological nightmare? It was getting late and I was beat. I decided to go to bed early since I wanted to have another go at it with Susan first thing the next morning. Perhaps another hypnosis session would yield some further information.

I called the hospital just before retiring for the evening, just to be sure that Susan wasn't having any further outbursts. All seemed quiet at the moment, according to the head nurse on the night shift. So I turned in, and as I drifted off to sleep, I kept thinking that in my field of medicine, some cases just never seem to find resolution. But I still was determined to help Susan in any way that I could.

Chapter 53

The next morning I was just as stumped as I was the day before about Susan's case. After breakfast, I called the nurses' station at the hospital to see if the night had been uneventful. Apparently, it hadn't gone very well. I was informed that Susan had first begun singing that song, *Blue Skies*. Then the screaming began, and according to the nurse, after Susan was medicated, she kept repeating that Charles was going to take her away. I told her I would be in soon to look in on Susan.

I kept thinking on the drive to the hospital that at some point in Susan's life there had to be some type of psychological trauma that was causing these disassociated outbursts, but for the life of me, I was completely mystified in understanding her loss of connection to the real world. I finally arrived at the hospital and picked up Susan's chart from the nurses' station on the way to my office, where I sat down and began going through the evening nurse's hand-written notes.

After I completed reading the notes, I decided to look in on Susan to determine just how coherent she might be before I attempted another hypnosis session. I asked Horace to join me as I opened the door to Susan's room. She seemed to be sleeping, so I said to Horace, "Let's leave her for now and we can try a little later. I'd rather have her get some much needed rest rather than disturb her now."

As Horace and I began walking back to the nurses'

station, we suddenly heard music that seemed to be coming from multiple directions. "Where the hell is that music coming from, Horace?" I asked.

"I honestly don't know, Dr. Morrissey. These long halls really echo. So it's hard to pinpoint where the sound is coming from."

"Let's take a walk, Horace. Do you recognize the melody?" I asked.

"Why yes, Dr. Morrissey. That's the same song that Susan is always singing. I think it's called *Blue Skies*."

"But where the hell is it coming from, Horace?" I asked again. As we began walking toward Susan's room, the music became louder. Then the moment Horace placed his key in the door, the music stopped abruptly.

As Horace opened the door to the room, we both were shocked at what we saw. Or rather what we didn't see. There was Susan's chair, a nightstand and her bed, but no patient. The restraints that had held Susan tied down to the bed were still in the bed, and the straps were still tied tightly to the bed's side rails. But there wasn't any sign of Susan at all.

"Horace, call Security immediately. We have to find her," I said.

"But Dr. Morrissey, she couldn't have gotten out, we just saw her not five minutes ago, and you saw me lock the door when we came out. This is insane," Horace said.

"I know, Horace, but get Security up here anyway. We have to find her somehow," I said.

Horace ran to the nurses' station and got Security on the phone. They were on the floor in less than a minute. They all were familiar with Susan and knew what she looked like. Protocol also required the hospital to contact the state police when a patient is missing, which we did, and they arrived in roughly fifteen minutes after the call was made.

All of us checked every patient room, along with every crack and crevice in the place, and still we couldn't find Susan. I provided a picture and description of Susan for the police, and they set off to cover the grounds of the hospital in the hopes of finding her. Something inside of me thought they never were going to locate her, but I didn't dare utter what I was thinking. I couldn't even believe it myself.

Chapter 54

As the state police were scouring the grounds of the hospital, I headed back to my office to inform Susan's parents about the events that were actively taking place. Olivia wasn't home, but Susan's father, Oscar, answered the phone.

"Oh my God! How did that happen? She has to be there somewhere! You've got to find her, Doctor! What can we do?"

"We are doing everything we can, Oscar. Would you and your wife like to come over to the hospital while we try to put together a strategy?" I asked Oscar.

"Of course we would. Olivia is visiting with a neighbor, but I will leave now and pick her up, and we will be there as fast as we can," he said, trying to contain his distress over the situation.

Just as I hung up from talking with Oscar a state police investigator knocked on my door and asked if I was Susan's doctor. I answered in the affirmative, and he asked if he could ask me some questions.

It was nearly an hour later when I finally had finished answering questions the investigator's questions. As he was leaving my office, a state trooper arrived and stated there was no sign of Susan on the hospital grounds. After they checked the patient's room once again, they were still baffled as to how she could have slipped out of her locked room. There was only one window in Susan's room, and it had bars on it, so she certainly couldn't have gotten out that way. I mentioned to the trooper that Susan was under four-point restraints, which she couldn't possibly have gotten out of unless she was Harry Houdini.

"Dr. Morrissey, is there any way she could have picked the lock on the door to her room?" the trooper asked.

"Absolutely not," I replied. "You'll notice that the only place a key can be used is on the outside of the door, and not in the patient's room. So there isn't any way that the lock could be picked from the inside," I said.

"Well, Dr. Morrissey, I'll leave a couple of officers to keep searching the hospital grounds, and hopefully we'll come up with at least some clue," the trooper said.

"Thank you for all your help. Susan's parents should be arriving soon, and this is a conversation I'm not looking forward to," I admitted.

I returned to my office and felt that I had in some way let down both Susan and her parents. How could this possibly have happened? Where in the world could she have gone? I closed the door to my office as the police left. I just needed a few minutes to process the events that had taken place.

People just don't disappear into thin air, and yet Susan was gone, and now I was going to have to relive these events with Susan's parents. For the first time in my career, I was at a total loss for any plausible explanation. At that moment my phone rang and it was the guard at the front desk asking if he could send Oscar and Olivia up to my office.

"Yes, please send them right up," I responded.

On the rare occasion when a patient died at the hospital, it was often simpler to console family members than in a case like this, as there was a body to be buried, and the family could have some type of closure. But how could there possibly be any closure for Susan's parents if we never found Susan? At this point I could not possibly explain her disappearance, and I dreaded admitting that to them.

Chapter 55

Several police officers were still going through Susan's room, dusting everything for any fingerprints or other forensic evidence that might be found. Meanwhile, I heard Olivia and Oscar walking down the hall toward my office. I knew this wasn't going to be easy, so I had asked the investigator I had spent the last hour with if he would join me when talking to Susan's parents.

"Please come in," I said to Susan's parents. "This is inspector Gerald, from the New York State Police.

"What happened?" Olivia and Oscar asked, almost in unison.

"Honestly, we don't really know at this point, other than your daughter is missing from a locked patient room," Inspector Gerald replied. "Susan has been here, from what Dr. Morrissey has told me, for the last fifteen years. Is that correct?"

"Yes, Inspector," Olivia said.

"Is there anyone that you might be aware of that might want to cause harm to your daughter?" the inspector asked.

"Why no," Oscar replied. "Our daughter has been here, as you said, for just over fifteen years, and was in the care of Dr. Morrissey."

"I hate bothering you folks, but I will have to get a bit more information about your daughter. May I stop by your home later this evening?" the inspector asked.

"Why of course you can," Oscar replied. "Let me write down the address for you."

"Dr. Morrissey, I'm going to head back to the office and I'll be in touch should I have any further questions."

"Thank you, Inspector Gerald. I'm available at any time should you need me," I said.

After the inspector left, Olivia asked how this possibly could have happened.

"Honestly, Olivia, we just don't know. There was a very strange event that had taken place, which I discussed with the police when they arrived. The orderly, Horace, and I heard a song that Susan always referred to, called *Blue Skies*. Does that mean anything to either of you," I asked.

"Why no, Dr. Morrissey," Olivia said.

"It was the strangest moment of my life. It was almost surreal," I commented.

"Where were you when this happened, Dr. Morrissey?" Oscar asked.

Horace and I were walking in the hallway, trying to find the source of the music. It seemed to get louder as we walked toward Susan's room. Her room was still locked, and then when Horace placed the key into the lock, the music immediately stopped. When we opened the door, Susan was gone. I wish I could explain this in some more coherent way, but honestly, I'm at a total loss as to what happened, or where Susan might be."

Oscar's voice grew louder as he said, "Well, Susan has to be here somewhere."

"I assure you, Oscar, that we're doing everything we can to find her," I said. "There really isn't anything else we can do at this point, but I know the police are continuing their search," I said.

"I hold you directly responsible for our missing daughter," Oscar said, accusingly, "and you'll be hearing from our attorney."

"Please, Folks. I know you're upset, but we will get to the bottom of this one way or the other," I said.

Neither of Susan's parents said another word and both got up and left my office in apparent contempt. *Who could blame them?* I thought to myself.

Chapter 56

I was standing outside of the Emergency Room as my shift as a third year psychiatric resident was nearly done. I had only an hour to go before I finally could get some sleep. Off in the distance, I could hear the sirens. I walked back inside the hospital and asked the charge nurse if she knew what was coming in.

"Sam, the only thing I know from the police scanner is that there was a multiple homicide, but they caught the guy, who they said is a total whack job, and that's who they're bringing in."

It wasn't long before the ambulance was backing in, and I could see two officers trying to wrestle some guy down on the ambulance stretcher.

"Taser him if you have to," one officer said to his partner. "This guy is totally crazy."

As I stood by the entrance, the police officers wheeled the stretcher into the Emergency Room. "Place him in bay number four," I said to one of the officers. "What have we got here, gentlemen?" I asked, as I noticed that the patient was covered in blood.

"We were called out for a multiple homicide," one of the officers replied. "We found both parents, their three daughters, a son and a male servant, all with multiple stab wounds. There was blood all over the place, and then we found this nut case hiding in a closet, clutching a butcher knife, with blood all over him."

I asked one of the officers how old the members of the family were.

"The mother and father looked to be in their mid-fifties. The daughters ranged probably from about seventeen or eighteen to maybe their mid-twenties, and the son probably was in his early thirties. I would guess the servant was in his mid-fifties. According to a British passport we found in his wallet, his name was Oscar Winthrop. The coroner should be finishing up soon and will be sending the bodies here for autopsies."

"What do you know about this guy we have here?" I asked.

"The only thing we know, based on items found in his wallet, is that his name is Charles Sycamore, and he's one of yours," the officer said.

"What do you mean, *one of mine?*" I asked.

"Well, according to his identification we found on him, he's a psychiatrist. I guess his case load finally drove him off the deep end," the officer said.

"Any idea who the family was?" I asked.

"From information we found at the scene, the father was Dr. David Morrissey, his wife's name was Olivia, and the children were Lila, Laura, Susan and Peter," the officer said.

"Wow, this guy must have just snapped. I wonder what the trigger was."

"That's your specialty, Doc," the officer said. "He's your problem now. I think we're done here for the time being, but we'll post an officer in his room," the officer said.

"Okay, Gentlemen. Thanks for making my night. I was supposed to be off soon and I guess that's going out the window."

"Never a dull moment, eh Doc?" one of the officers observed, as they left to return to duty.

The only thing that could be done with a patient in this much of an agitated state was to start an IV line and begin administering benzodiazepine to calm him down, but at the same time keeping him in the handcuffs he came in with. I was just too tired to get into the patient's history, as sketchy as it was. The police didn't have that much information on him, but there was no doubt that the detectives that were walking in now wanted some answers.

Detective Cameron approached me and asked if I was the attending physician.

"No, I'm the on-call resident, Dr. Sam Richmond." I replied. "How can I help you?"

"I'd like to talk to your patient, if that's possible."

"It's going to have to wait until later in the morning. We have him heavily sedated at this point. Do you have any background on this patient other than what happened this evening?" I asked.

Detective Cameron began to explain: "Dr. Charles Sycamore had been in a long-standing professional argument with Dr. Morrissey. What ever happened, Sycamore lost his license and basically his livelihood several years ago, and always blamed Dr. Morrissey for his troubles. It appears he just snapped and decided to kill not only the doctor, but his entire family, as well as the British male servant, which probably was his butler."

"I might check with my chief of staff," I suggested. He may have further information on both of these doctors."

"Well, any further information will help our

investigation. Please give me a call when we can finally talk with the perpetrator," he said, as he held out his card to me through two fingers.

"I certainly will, Detective Cameron," I replied, as I took his card.

At this point the patient was being transferred to the lockdown unit, and I would follow up after I had the chance to get some much-needed sleep. It wasn't much of a stretch in questioning the patient's sanity. But I couldn't imagine what would have pushed Dr. Sycamore to take the action he did.

Epilogue

As long as I live, I doubt I will ever forget the night that the police brought in Dr. Charles Sycamore. It was that time of the month where case reviews took place with the head of the Psychiatry Department, Dr. William Lewis. The case of Dr. Sycamore was truly a sad one. Here was a man that was at the top of his game and then his world simply collapsed. He had been hospitalized several times over the last six months, to no avail.

Dr. Sycamore had apparently gotten into a professional argument with Dr. Morrissey over unorthodox treatment methodologies, and was ultimately brought up on professional charges of misconduct with a patient. Dr. Morrissey was on the states medical review board, and it was his decision to revoke Dr. Sycamore's license permanently. That pretty much killed his career. Some associates came forward to the police and stated that after losing his ability to practice, he just went off the deep end.

After Dr. Sycamore lost his license, he began drinking heavily, and like some in the field of medicine, he began to self-medicate, using a variety of drugs. Mixed with alcohol, and you have a prescription for disaster. Over time, friends and family said he was becoming highly delusional. He would create fantasies in his mind using Dr. Morrissey's family members.

Even in the twenty-first century there seems to be much

we don't understand about the human mind and its interactions with our emotions. What is it, I wondered, that takes place in our daily lives that ignites these emotional triggers that could bring a professional like Dr. Sycamore to kill an entire family?

There wasn't any doubt in my mind that Dr. Sycamore would be found incapable of standing trial. From a medical perspective, as well as in the eyes of the court, he eventually would be found to be clinically insane, and probably remanded to a state psychiatric facility for the rest of his life, only to be forgotten in time.

One unusual aspect of this case was Dr. Sycamore's obsession with an old tune from the 1930's called *Blue Skies.* After doing a little research and talking to some of Dr. Sycamore's extended family members, apparently the song, *Blue Skies,* was his wife's favorite song from their wedding.

After the doctor lost his license to practice medicine, his wife said he fell into a terrible state of depression and then became delusional. She said he heard voices and at times would be found in their living room having arguments with the voices in his head. His wife tried anything that would have cheered him up, even playing their favorite song. But on the last occasion she had played it for him, he went into a violent rage and stormed out of his home saying he never ever wanted to hear that melody again.

How scary a thought it is, being trapped in one's mind! How does an individual fight his demons without the need to take another human life, let alone seven, in this case? Without question, medicine is both an art as well as a science, and yet to this very day, there is so much left to understand when it comes to the human mind.

We had gone as far as we could with Dr. Sycamore, and his fate would now be left up to a jury of his peers. I doubted I ever would have a final answer, but I did wonder how Dr. Sycamore became so entrenched with his multiple personalities and his fixation on these characters that he created in his own mind. I thought for the moment that my chosen field had a very long way to go before that conundrum was ever to be solved.

As I closed the Sycamore file, I was looking out a window in our conference room. As I stood watching everyday people go about their everyday existence, I just wondered how many more Sycamores would be coming through our Emergency Room doors in the months and years to come.

Whoever fights monsters should see to it
that in the process he does not become a monster.
And if you gaze long enough into the abyss,
the abyss will gaze back into you.

Frederick Nietzsche